CW00695911

Vicki Hastrich lives in Sydney, in a house with three hot water systems.

SWIMMING
with the JELLYFISH

SWIMMING
with the JELLYFISH

VICKI HASTRICH

SCRIBNER

SWIMMING WITH THE JELLYFISH
First published in Australia in 2001 by Scribner
an imprint of Simon & Schuster (Australia) Pty Limited
20 Barcoo Street, East Roseville NSW 2069

A Viacom Company
Sydney New York London Toronto Singapore

National Library of Australia
Cataloguing-in-Publication data:

Hastrich, Vicki.
Swimming with the Jellyfish.

ISBN 0 7318 1064 3.

I. Title

A823.4

Cover design by Yolande Gray
Cover image by Warwick Orme
Typeset by Asset Typesetting Pty Ltd in 11/14 Sabon
Printed in Australia by Griffin Press

10 9 8 7 6 5 4 3 2 1

For Paul,
and in memory of
a house on a hill.

ACKNOWLEDGMENTS

Many people have helped along the way in the making of this novel. My thanks to Sue Woolfe who gave me a beginning and a means to continue, and to Judith Lukin-Amundsen, Lyn Tranter, Julia Stiles, Kim Swivel and Jody Lee variously for their expertise and advice.

I am grateful to the Eleanor Dark Foundation, the NSW Ministry for the Arts and the Australia Council for the important experience of attending Varuna – the Writers' House in the Blue Mountains – via fellowship and mentorship programmes.

Extra special thanks to the executive director of Varuna, the lovely Peter Bishop, who has been a true friend to the *Jellyfish*. His skilled reading and his care and his undamped enthusiasm have resuscitated this book many times over.

More than anyone else, my smart, funny and enduring writing friends, Eileen Naseby, Rebecca Hazel and Charlotte Wood, have been essential to the process and I cannot thank them enough for all they have done, together and individually.

Thanks to dear Patrick and all the Clarks, and, lastly, thanks to my own patient family. See, I wasn't fibbing all that time – I was writing a novel.

CONTENTS

PROLOGUE
THE WHOLE TOWN SLEEPS

I turn the flowers back, it feels like opening an envelope; I turn the counterpane of flowers back onto Davey's empty side of the bed. There is nothing to be had in this room. No sleep. At the window with the curtains parted round me like a nun's veil there's no breeze. But from far away over, a long way over, I can hear the sea. Its shush and boom comes if I hold my breath. The lawn is empty except for rust falling on outdoor furniture.

I will go for a walk.

I am walking. Through the town in my nightie. With a cardigan slung round my shoulders and my cracked heels hanging over the edges of a pair of scuffs. I follow the hollow call of the surf, it seems the only thing to do, taking slow steps up the hill. The houses, with their dark sloping yards, are all tucked in. I imagine all the people I know in this town and how they'll be sleeping: Davey, self-exiled and finally unconscious, with his mouth open and the soft eye of his dick snoozing out of the fly in his pyjama pants; Rosie Lunt lying neat as a pin with the covers pulled up to her chin; Question Mark Man dangled like a spider over the arms of his vinyl chair in front of the TV, and Black Dog curled nose to tail twitching with dreams; the oysterman turned to the wall in a foetal pose and muttering the echo of a Methodist prayer; Viv in an apple-green negligee facing away from Ray but with one foot kicked back and hooked over his ankle; Dad, maybe asleep in his clothes, but not forgetting his ritual with the pillows – the two of them laid carefully end to end under the blankets, like sausage meat in pastry, to fill the place where Mum had been; Janet Constable and Iris and Bertie Marchant sprawled in an exhausted threesome. The whole town snores. How do they all stay wedged in their beds when it seems a careless nudge has tipped the world on its side and everything of mine is tumbling out of cupboards?

I am the only sleepwalker.

The kerb and guttering give way to gravel and crumble-edged bitumen. Christmas lights blink in the lounge room window of the last house before the crest. Over the hill, a salt-heavy mist hangs in the air. I can taste it on my lips. Houses sprinkle down to a fringe near the beach. The car park at the surf club floats ahead, street lights leaning over it. It's a deserted sporting arena, jewel-flecked with broken glass and flattened beer bottle tops, confettied with condom packets.

I take the dark track through the dunes. The world at night, without colour, is a muffled place. The only thing for sure is the grey-white foam of the surf, its treacherous lace strung right the way up the beach. I would not swim in the dark. It would make me feel like a lost soul to swim in the dark.

I sit in the damp sand well back from the water, hunkered down with my nightie pulled over my knees. Crack, boom, boom of the surf. But I have company. Up at the Heights *there's a dull glow of orange coming from one of the cliff-top houses. I bet Barbara Audette's behind that light, smoking endless cigarettes in her cathedral gloom, watching the waves and shadows as I do.*

She's waiting with me.

We are awake together on the night the whole town sleeps as if it's taken a potion.

We'll wait for daybreak.

CHAPTER ONE

SOMETHING IN THE WATER

I'm waiting my turn for the dentist and the dentist's father is with me.

'Gum leaves,' he says. 'Aboriginal persons used to chew the leaves of eucalypt trees to clean their teeth. That is why they are called gum leaves. If you are ever without a brush or tube of toothpaste then simply pick a leaf.'

He goes from straightening the magazines, to the seat next to me, to the filing cabinet behind the reception desk, he can't stay still.

'Bacteria does not exist in an active form in the frozen wastes of the polar icecaps.' Now he's sitting in the receptionist's chair and only his head is visible above the high benchtop. His voice is very loud. 'This is therefore the only place on earth where it is not necessary for man to brush daily.'

I select a *National Geographic* magazine hoping I can pretend to be too busy to listen to more of this lecture. But I've chosen badly and immediately I'd like to put it back; there are Eskimos on the front cover framed with that bright-for-science yellow and they look sad. The Eskimos, dressed in fur which sticks out wide as porcupine needles, are standing outside an icehouse (they must bend low to make it through the doorway), and there's an unattractive hole of brown water in front of them, as if the ocean has gone off. Perhaps it has.

'Killer whales,' says the dentist's father, suddenly materialising at my shoulder and staring at the magazine, 'killer whales, for all their black-and-white striped ferocity, are renowned as being the marine mammals with the weakest teeth.'

I didn't know that.

'You didn't know that, did you?' he says, sticking his face right into mine. '*Orcinus orca* does not require strong teeth because he has them by the plenty. Row upon row of them in constant manufacture. If the human head were blessed with comparable sets then, due to lack of space, our tongues would be reduced to cockatoo size.'

I didn't know that either. He removes his face from mine and I refix my gaze on the magazine. Past advertisements for binoculars and American Express cards, the Eskimos reappear. Now they are getting out of a snowmobile which is parked outside a church. It is a picture grey with falling snow and only the yellow headlights of the vehicle provide colour. I don't know whether it's day or night. 'Inuit: New Days and Old Ways', says the title through the snow.

'The study of primates in their wild state has contributed much to *homo sapiens* sociology,' announces the dentist's father.

How did he get from fish to apes? He clears his throat and takes up a central position in the middle of the waiting room.

'As part of a recognition ritual, orang-utans sniff each other nose to mouth. If unhygienic odours are detected the offending individual is shunned until the problem has been redressed by the vigorous chewing of tubers. Why? Why are apes, who are, after all, content to live with fleas, so sensitive to halitosis?'

Don't ask me. But he's boring a stare straight into my eyes demanding an answer. He taps his shoe, waiting, but I can't think of a thing to say until he finally gives up and continues with exaggerated huffs, 'Because the baring of teeth signals both aggression and desire. If teeth are missing or otherwise marred by decay the animal is deemed to be weak and unhealthy. Such a sorry beast would be unable to attract a partner.'

The dentist's father shakes his head with woe-betide sadness.

'Oral hygiene,' he brightens up, seeing the triumph of his conclusion looming, 'is thus crucial to the continuation of the species, and it is for this reason that the group maintains such vigilance on individual standards.'

He seems pleased with himself and smiles benignly at the far corner of the room as if expecting some applause from this quarter. Just as I return meekly to the pages of my magazine, thinking I'm dismissed, he wheels on me again and prods the air.

'BUT, how does the ape world provide a window through which to view the human race?'

My heart sinks in direct relation to the speed with which he jabs his forefinger.

'Consider a young man's smile to a pretty girl. Is this not the first overture of sexual interest?'

Now he's onto sex! Any minute he'll ask me something about a cervix and I won't know.

'Strong societies are populous societies and populous societies have strong teeth. Look at the Chinese peoples. Predominantly rice eaters, they possess magnificent chompers since their teeth are rarely defiled by sugar loaded foods. And the result – they have population to burn!'

He throws his arms out wide as if to demonstrate the enormity of the pyre which would be required to do this.

'The lesson is simple,' he finishes, 'Clean your teeth or perish!'

A door opens and shuts down the hall and the dentist's father sidles into the chair next to mine; he becomes suddenly leery.

'What are you in for?' he whispers.

'A cavity,' I say.

Footsteps arrive in the waiting room. It's the receptionist.

'Mr Pool,' she says, 'how about a cup of coffee?'

She lures him away with the promise of a bun and sends me a look of sympathy.

Right now I can think of better ways to spend an afternoon off work. My nerves are already ragged. Thankfully, the typeface of the *National Geographic* looks balanced and reassuring. I rest myself in the print and avoid the pictures. I don't want to look at anyone's mouth and know the future of their family line. The stuff about traditional Eskimo ways turns out to be absorbing and in the end I have to rush to finish the last bit because the receptionist is back and it's my turn to go in.

I amble down the hall, is anyone ever in a hurry to face the drill, and glance into the first room. It's an X-ray area and has a 1950s science-fiction-Bakelite look. As I turn back, there, one foot from my face, is the dentist's father.

With the round vowels of a Vincent Price he says, 'Allow me,' and he escorts me to the surgery door. As he opens it he leans towards me and hisses in my ear so that I feel the warm puffs of his breath, *'Your mother was a whore and your father watched.'*

'Thanks, Dad,' says the dentist.

My mouth is agape like the hinges are broken.

'You can wait until you're in the chair,' says the dentist, pointing at my open mouth. He waves me further into the small bright room.

'Hope Dad didn't bother you,' he smiles. 'My wife usually looks after him but they had a bit of a tiff yesterday and I thought I'd better bring him in. He loves it here.'

My tongue, much smaller than cockatoo size, is struggling for words.

'... Was he a dentist too?'

The son shakes his head.

'A zoo keeper?'

'No.' And he giggles as if he's been tickled, this angular, kind man. 'He was a fitter and turner by trade but he always wished he'd been a teacher.'

'He's very, um, impressive. He knows a lot.'

'He used to, he educated himself,' says the dentist, stooping to soap up his soft hands in the little white wash-basin, 'but unfortunately his memory's gone so he makes up a lot.'

'My father's memory might be going a bit funny,' I say. 'He's done a few things recently that have sort of worried me.'

'Well, it's the short-term memory that's the first to go. Dad's pretty scrambled now but he often remembers things that happened years ago with a hundred per cent pinpoint accuracy.'

I gulp. 'Is that so?'

Your mother was a whore and your father watched.

The dentist adjusts the sucker thing in my mouth.

'Oh yes, names, dates, the lot.'

I wince.

'Don't worry – this scraping is just going to be a loud noise in your head.'

The dentist has a very nice plaster rosette in the middle of the ceiling directly above this chair. I wonder if he ever lies back here, maybe for a rest after lunch, and looks up, past the headlight glare of the lamp, into the creamy folds of decoration. It's a handy thing to concentrate on while your lips are being stretched in three directions and your mouth is full of metal tools. There's a comfort in the order of the formal shapes. It looks cool, it could be sculptured ice.

You know, in that magazine it said that inside an igloo it's warm enough to take off all your clothes – walk around in the nude. Mind you, if you're an Eskimo your clothes are things like shirts made out of a hundred birds and trousers of polar bear fur. I reckon you'd want to take off your clothes because they'd get itchy. And you'd need to look after them because new clothes would be pretty hard to come by. No shops – you trudge out on the winter pack-ice in the dark and kill your bear, I don't know how, and then you drag it all the way home, still in the dark, an Arctic wind screaming to be let in the holes of your old suit, minus 54 degrees (wind chill factored in). And probably you must sing some North Pole song through chattering teeth to thank a spirit for what seems only relative good luck. And should you forget to do this simple thing then maybe the ice will rear and split and you and your bear will disappear. The crack will close and there will be no trace that you were ever there in the endless icy waste.

Actually, it's a bit rude to call it a waste. I mean, it's not a waste if you know what to do with it. And, after all, your home's your home, you're stuck with it.

'Lal?'

'— Oh. Yes. Pardon?' And I suddenly realise I can open and close my mouth unimpeded by medical steel and suction things.

'You can rinse now.'

I go and pay, talking carefully through my frozen face like someone practising ventriloquism. The dentist's father is lurking with a feather duster, dabbing at the 'Sorry no cheques' sign. I'm scratching round in my purse for the cash, thinking I'm sure I had another fifty dollar note tucked away.

'Money just disappears these days,' says the receptionist to hide my embarrassment.

'I don't know what I've spent it on half the time,' she says.

'Well that's the truth,' I say and I drag out the note which was stuck behind a lotto ticket.

'There's a little bit of truth in everything,' pipes up the dentist's father and he looks me fair in the eye and winks. So smug he might have just swallowed a Persian cat and all her kittens and especially enjoyed digesting the fur.

Your mother was a whore.

* * *

The bus home from Coolie is slow. It's always slow since a fair percentage of the journey involves the headache-inducing use of low gears to climb uphill. The road finally levels out along the coastal ridge and then it drops quickly to the last stop – my stop – Pocket Head. I spend the long eight miles staring out the bus window the way I always do; inlet glimpses, houses, trees, Five Wells, more bush and trees, the odd intersecting road. Only today I don't feel so well.

When I get off the bus I walk past the only shop, past my street, and on to Dad's. I call out at the back door and go on in to find him in the front room, elaborately set up. He's got the traymobile pulled up to his chair as a workbench. Flux and metal scraps and rags and wire and Blu-Tack spread about. A set of windchimes is laid out with care as if it is a jellyfish whose tendrils require repair.

I slump in the chair opposite. It's lumpy-bottomed and awful but I can't sit in the other always-empty one. It was Mum's. Looking at Dad, I'm disturbed by the strangeness of his work but I tell myself it's okay, he's okay, this is nothing compared to the antics of the dentist's father.

My lips are numb and rubbery. One whole side of my face is a blank from the left nostril right up to a cold nub of ear-lobe. I could be wearing half a mask. I am heavy-hearted. Maybe those drugs can get to other parts of your body but, if I'm honest, it's not really the anaesthetic that's got to me, it's the dentist's father, and what he said to me. For ages, really quite long periods of time, I can be matter-of-fact about what happened to my mother, I keep it clamped, it takes some effort, life goes on, but then some small incident jabs up out of the blue and I am forced to take quick glances at it all again. The questions surface, the familiar pangs begin, spikes of grief pain. I want to know, I don't want to know, I have no way of knowing what happened to my mother. Old Mr Pool's not likely to give me a sensible answer, is he? Could he? I don't want to know.

Dad turns his contraption over and potters from piece to piece with quiet and methodical purpose. It was his birthday last week and I gave him the chimes to sing him some company. My husband, Davey, reckoned it was a rotten present for a bloke, but Dad seemed pleased enough. He admired the workmanship, the weights and balances of tones as he put his fingers through the curtain of tubes. Davey helped him fix them to the eaves outside the window. But now, after only a week, here they are splayed out on the traymobile undergoing an operation.

'In the gas company,' Dad's saying, 'efficiency was not necessarily a good thing.'

'Dad,' I say, pressing at my nostril to see if any feeling's returned, 'what dentist do you go to?'

'Armitage.'

'Not Pool?'

'No, never been to Pool. Pass me those scissors, will you? Is he a young fella?'

'No, he's older than me. I thought you might have known his father.'

'A modification, Lallie, can sometimes …' he ties a knot, '… work wonders.'

'Did you know him? The father?'

'Pool?'

'Yeah, he says he knows you.'

'I don't think so.'

But Dad's not concentrating on my questions. He's

peering at the smoking point of the soldering iron and I know he's not listening properly.

'You might know him. He was a fitter and turner.'

'No,' he says. 'I never knew a Pool at all, not him or his son.'

And just the way he dips the solder in the flux with such a fussy care for that and nothing else makes me think this is the truth. He didn't know a Pool.

But did a Pool know him?

To distract myself I get out the ironing board and push it in close to the window. There're a few things of Dad's that need doing. I love the cosiness of this front room. It's a closed-in verandah which gives the house a bit of a blank-faced look from the outside, but when you're inside it's like a picture frame for the view of the inlet. While the iron heats up I pick up Dad's binoculars and scan the bay, bumping over the water until I isolate a putt-putt motorboat. I keep moving with it, giving it a little bit of open water to cut into. What I've got before my eyes is a rudimentary image, as if from the early days of film, when ordinary objects became marvellous again just because they moved. In the grainy magnification, there's a simple uncluttered truth. It's just a picture of a boat moving through water, and it's lovely.

I whip the binoculars round the bay making the world blur and then pull up suddenly. I've got myself an eyeful of Merrengong rooftops, red tiles and painted iron, the gable of the old iceworks, a forest of television aerials spiking up tall to catch the best of a bad signal. Whip and blur again. The oysterman's house. It's lonely in the picture, crouched at the base of steep bush which leans over it. It's no more than a tumbledown shack really, a foxhole. I see him, in this late afternoon, come out with a bucket of probably chook scraps. He disappears with it behind the outhouse. He moves quickly, as if spending too much time in the open is poor strategy, as if eyes like mine could pick him off and do him harm. His yellow weatherboard cottage is stained where mud from the gutters has streaked black down the walls. When he ducks back inside it seems too flimsy to give him cover, too cranny-bored by draughts to keep him warm. The oysterman lives in full view of us and we forget he's even there, although there's no mistaking him if you should be in the corner shop when he makes one of his rare visits.

I remember him embarrassing Mum and me one day. Well, it was me who had been embarrassed – I was a teenager and everything made me cringe. We'd walked into the shop and there he was mumbling and passing a list to Mrs Grattan, the lady who owned it then, and attached to him was the usual plume of odour, the lethal combination of low-tide mud and unwashed skin. We kept well clear and headed towards the magazine rack. Mrs Grattan packed up a box of goods and had just asked the old man for the money – he seemed old even then – when in swaggered a bunch of local boys. The shop was suddenly full of testosterone.

'Er phew, who shat themselves?' they called out while the oysterman fumbled and dropped the change. He struggled to pick it up with shaking fingers while the boys tried to push each other closer to him. 'Hey, Mrs, do you sell pegs in here?'

Mum went over and helped the oysterman gather the

coins and she held his dirty hand as she paid the money into it. He seemed to freeze. The fine fingers of a woman touching his cut-scarred hand. He was transfixed by the strangeness of it. Staring at her white wrist as if it belonged to a creature he'd never seen before.

Hoots and whistles.

The oysterman scrambled for the door.

On reflection, I'm still embarrassed. I'm embarrassed now because I didn't help pick up the money too.

I damp down one of Dad's shirts with the water bottle and set to with the iron. After thinking about the oysterman the warm smell of clean cotton is heavenly. I do the collar and move on to the back of the shirt. I like doing the backs best, it's where the whole garment starts to come under your control and you get to take the iron in wide hypnotic arcs as a change from the straight up and down. As I come to do the sleeves I see one cuff is beginning to fray and two buttonholes on the front are torn. I take the iron away.

'This one's had it, Dad,' I say. 'Time to pitch it.'

He looks up from his operation on the wind chimes and frowns over his spectacles. 'Ah, not that one, love, it's a beauty.'

I give my cheek a Three Stooges slap but it's still cold as concrete.

Davey thinks I'm paranoid looking out for signs of Dad's mind becoming unravelled – after all, he isn't that old – but you lose one parent holus-bolus and you don't want to lose the other by degrees. After today, I'm seriously beginning to wonder if there's something in the water that eventually sends all the old men dotty round here, and, when you think about it, it's not something new. The oysterman had a father who went the whole hog and really flipped his lid. The thing is, he was an unpleasant man. They say he kept his wife and son almost prisoners in that mangrove-dark arm of the inlet. Wouldn't even let the boy go to school until a truant officer threatened the law and arranged for the Methodists to pick him up each day in the mission boat. But just because the bad man had a suitably bad end that's no reason to dismiss the story neatly. What about his poor son looking on? If you ask me, it turns you raw, seeing a parent crumble or get taken away.

Imagine the oysterman, barely more than a boy, watching from the front door of the yellow cottage. I want to touch his shoulder or squeeze his hand as he watches his father skip – nude – in the knee-deep water out of the valley shade into a spotlight of midwinter sun. The old man's raucous laughter disgusts the boy more than the unfamiliar sight of all that white father's flesh, cauliflower bottom and lolling doodle. The old man laughing, as if he always knew how.

After they tied the father up in a blanket and carted him off, I imagine the oysterboy standing in the doorway of that house for days, not knowing what to do next. Where once it took a day's labour to navigate the troughs of his father's moods, now there is time. I see him finally climb into his wooden boat and take up the oars, rowing the slate mornings of winter and the opal of summer afternoons, inscribing himself on the inlet. They have taken his father and with him all chances for change. He's a boy preserved. Missing the little he had and lonely for hate. Creak of rowlock and oar.

Lay low, lay low. These are the secrets of a boy who would become an oyster farmer.

There's something about the sea, about being born within sound of the sea, that binds you to it. Its rhythms put you in leg-irons. Lay low, lay low, you are hobbled to the sea.

I've almost come to the bottom of the second basket of clothes when Dad says into the empty air, 'That should just about do it,' and holds up the wind chimes. They binkle and bong in muted tones and the music is more beautiful for the notes they don't strike, for the ones he's removed. In his tinkering on the traymobile he has somehow made a melody of absence.

The steam iron puffs. It might be a sigh. The smell of impregnated sweat rises, sweet as marzipan.

Your father watched.

CHAPTER TWO

AT THE BOWLING CLUB

I'm hiding. Which is pretty hard to do when you're a large-arse in a lemon uniform on a bar stool.

I'm hiding behind Friday-night blooms of cigarette smoke and the bread smell of beer. Crossing my fingers that the noise of clattering glasses, drinkers' calls and poker machines will make a jagged screen of distractions to divert my enemy's gaze. As a last line of defence nothing can beat the Chef's Specials, so I'm holding up a takeaway menu high, pretending rapt attention, a difficult choice between the Szechuan Chicken and the Szechuan Prawns.

I'm hiding from Peggy O'Farrel.

You wouldn't think it necessary to go to so much trouble to avoid a woman who wears plastic bobble earrings and matching beads. But she's not as harmless as she appears.

Mai Yong, who runs the dining room, pokes her head out of the servery hatch behind the bar and calls out, 'You ordering early, Lal?' I shake my head and grimace no, ducking down deeper into the menu.

Polar bears are masters of camouflage. Just by wearing white. Their fur can change a thousand subtle hues reflected up from ice. If I was a polar bear I'd be safe from Peggy

O'Farrel. After my visit to the dentist I've been thinking a lot about Arctic things. And disappearing.

Peggy's over at the other side of the room now with her back to me, silhouetted by the green verandah light shining down over the glass front doors. She's leaning to talk into Rosie Lunt's right ear, and Rosie nods but her eyes flick from time to time to the collapsing froth on the top of her glass of pilsener, which is parked just out of polite reach on the edge of the bar. Davey and his mates at the pool table roar when one of them accidentally pockets the black. Peggy leans in further over little Rosie.

Peggy's the sort of person who gets you in a headlock with the sheer strength of her brick-veneer niceness. She bailed me up outside the corner shop last night, inviting me to join the Stitch and Bitch Club. Before I had a chance to murmur, she ran on, 'It's on at Joy's house next week. We have a lot of fun and we'd love to have you with us.'

I said it didn't sound all that fun – having to darn your husband's socks and talk about him. I wasn't trying to be funny but she laughed and said, 'No, you just bring along a handicraft and talk, well, girl sort of talk.'

That made me think of ovarian cysts.

When I was young the small-town press-gangs were continually at me to come and belong to this thing or that club. It marked your passage through time. Brownies, Ballet, Girl Guides, Eisteddfod Choir. I used to be a sucker and could not resist.

'You don't like to sing out loud,' Mum had said. 'You're a hummer. They'll expect to hear more than humming, you know.'

But then when I grew up, the Peggys and her type

gradually let me be. One by one they drifted off, as if following an individual scent that led to a common stream, and had children of their own. I was ignored in their busyness, 'Can't stop, must fly,' they said as they rushed to weigh their babies at the Baby Health. They answered the telephone with pins in their mouths, 'I'm sewing on Boy Scout badges,' they explained, talking carefully through stretched lips so as not to take an uncomfortable mouthful. They left me alone, departing from conversations, saying, 'Aren't you lucky you don't have children,' and not really meaning it. Me not feeling lucky at all.

But now they're coming back. We're all at the wrong end of our thirties now and their kids are becoming independent, they've got time on their hands, and they're turning their attention to me. They're ratting the fridge for me, like I'm leftovers, with flavours remembered as puzzling and not fully explored.

I watch Peggy's jaw move up and down as she talks to Rosie and, though she's probably saying something innocuous, I imagine she's recounting to Rosie what she said to me: 'We won't take no for an answer, Lal. We'll wear you down.'

She said it with an eye-twinkle. Hunters' glee.

Crash of glass.

'Bastard!'

Dining room commotion.

It's Mai.

She's going off at Bobby Goggle-Eyes, the club waiter. He drives her crazy, 'Piece of noodle smarter than you!'

For Mai, every slip of Bobby's gross motor skills is a threat to her survival. I've heard her on the topic a million times before. She reckons for sure he'll knock over a candle one day and set fire to the tablecloths and burn down her restaurant and then how will she feed her kids and pay off her house and look after her mother and get her husband a digital television set and repay the longstanding sponsorship debt she owes to the old branch of the family that brought her out to Australia in the first place? She comes barging through the dining room swing doors now, pushing Bobby ahead of her like she's rolling a stone, doing her best to hurry the unhurryable Bobby out of her domain. She's hitting him with a tea towel and swearing in two languages plus maybe a third. Bobby blinks behind his thick spectacles and concentrates on steadying his tray full of broken bottles. There's a red wine stain on his white shirt in the perfect shape of a reindeer and it's the only thing about him that's not dishevelled. Some bloke yells out, 'Hey, Mai, pick on someone your own size,' and heaps of people laugh because she's only five foot three. She spots me and comes over to my corner of the bar mopping her brow with the tea towel but glowing and refreshed as if she'd just finished a satisfying workout at the gym. She points to the menu and my strange posture. 'What's going on?'

'I'm hiding,' I say.

'It's not working,' she says. 'You are as obvious as one horse in a paddock.' She waves her hand as if I'm half mad but also in a so-what-it-doesn't-worry-her way and goes back into the dining room. If they weren't so busy I'd follow her and hang out in the kitchen drinking cups of Chinese green tea.

In the chaos of that kitchen there's a permanent still point and it's Mai's mother. I'd like to be like her. She has the face of faith. Broad and flat and smiling with barely a wrinkle. Her grey hair is tightly knotted back and she always wears a colourful apron round her thickening waist. The apron is small and looks about as useful as a hanky. I have never seen it smeared with grease or food from the loads of plates she handwashes in the deep sink.

Mother Lin smiles and works so fast you never see her hurry. And she does not speak.

On hot days she sits on the porch steps of their house, fanning herself while the little kids play round her on their bikes in the front yard. When dusk falls she may slap her bare ankles lazily after a mosquito but while the children are happy she does not move. There is nothing more important to get up for. Cradled in her lap is all the time in the world.

My own mother did not stay in the one spot like Mother Lin.

My own mother disappeared.

I turned fifteen. Two months later there was a note on the kitchen table.

Dear John and Lallie,
Have to go. Back as soon as I can.
Love, Mum.

It was like she'd forgotten to buy the milk or the bread and had ducked off to the shops.

For a long time after the note I would come home and go straight to the fridge, hoping there'd be more milk in there than when I'd left in the morning. And then I'd open up the back door. Maybe she'd be in the yard pegging out the washing, the basket at her feet. My socks. Dad's shirt. Her bra. She'd have her back to me, the wind jamming the skirt of her dress between her slim legs, the tethered clothes flapping away from her, straining and cracking like a spinnaker looking for a trustworthy gust. As she bent down for another piece of clothing she'd look up and see me in the doorway. She'd smile and say, 'Hello, love,' and I wouldn't hear the words because the wind had taken them away but I'd know she'd said them.

Do you ever go into the kitchen, purposefully because you're busy, and open a cupboard door and suddenly you're lost? You're staring at the shelves thinking what did I want in here. What am I doing here? And everything seems unfamiliar. And then you realise you've just gone to the wrong cupboard.

When Peggy O'Farrel left me at the shop last night she was all firm smiles. 'I don't give up easily, Lal,' she said.

Girl sort of talk. They're hunting me for my mother's secret and my shame is that I don't even know it to tell. They want something good, expect something big, they speculate, and sizzling on their matrons' lips is the word 'adultery'. That is the tale they'd prefer. My family naked before their gaze.

I can only do what I've always done, I'll fence them out.

My wrists are getting sore from holding up the menu.

Rosie nods.

Peggy nods.

Peggy departs and heads towards the Ladies. Hallelujah, I get to take a rest.

Rosie picks up her glass of pilsener and wriggles her beaded handbag down to the crook of her arm; compact, she's underway, making for a table near the feature brick wall under the television set. Her handbag swings, keeping time with her rolling gait. It's the uncharted sea of old age which makes her sway, which has frozen her ankle joints and set her rocking. As she passes by she nods at my uniform, 'How's work?' she grunts in her raspy voice, but doesn't wait for an answer. I don't blame her. There's nothing interesting about spending all your days with your hands in rubber gloves making sandwiches at a lunch shop in Coolie.

Rosie's one I've done ironing for. I iron for Dad but sometimes I iron for other people. It's come to be a thing I can help people with. Over the years things happen in families, someone's sick or has another baby; well, I might knock on their door and offer to do their ironing for them – just as a kindness – so that's one small task out of the way for them. Funny, but it does make a difference. I know as well as anybody what it's like to have your life plonked upside down and turned inside out and I've seen how people can be very strong at coping with the big stuff but they'll soon crack when they can't keep control of the ordinary things as well. People don't cry when they're snatching up pyjamas and toiletries for a hospital bag, they cry after they've delivered it, when they come home and there's a big pile of washing-up and a fly in the jam jar because the lid's been left off in haste. They cry because there's a fly in the jam jar and there shouldn't be.

When Rosie slipped on the path at the back of her house and broke her right arm we became friends. She'd been in plaster for a fortnight when I wheeled my washing trolley down our driveway and Davey came flapping out of the front door calling out, 'Where are you going with that thing?'

'Lunts'. And then Dad's,' I said.

'You can't go driving down the street with that. People are going to want to know if you've got a licence.'

I pretended I couldn't hear him and kept trolleying up the road, little stones making the wheels wobble.

'If anyone sees you, I'm dead meat,' he yelled. 'They'll take the piss out of me at the Lions Club.'

I took Rosie with me round to Dad's so she could have a change of scenery and we could all chat. She told us stories about her dead husband, Royce, and how it made her sick the way he always ate ice-cream with a knife and fork. After I walked her back home that afternoon she admired the crispness of my work and paused at her front door saying, 'You turned out a nice girl, Lal. Thank you.'

She had the hall light switched on behind her so I couldn't see her face in the half dark. But it was as if, maybe, she was a bit surprised.

Alone at her table now, she takes her glasses and a pen out of her handbag and combs through the pages of a little pocketbook, making small adjustments to the figures written there. She keeps a tally of all her poker machine profits and losses, trying to find out the best payers.

The door of the Ladies squeaks to signal the return of a relieved Peggy and unless she's got something stuck in her eye she's bound to spot me. All I can do is swing my head towards the wall and study the noticeboard. The bar noise drops away. My skin goes cold. The noticeboard – it's town voodoo. All of Pocket Head's activities and people and events are pinned there, haphazard pastings of who we are and what we do. Squares of paper moved to make room for more, overlapped, stuck with coloured pins; all that represents the town and makes it breathe. It breathes without me.

One horse in a paddock.

A pool of silence.

Where's my make-up mirror, I want to get it out and put its silvered surface to my mouth and nose – exhale – worried that it mightn't mist over. Palefaced, that's me, I'm a poor shell. But even crabs and crayfish can change their shells. Look at the noticeboard, the whole town changes itself over and again, everyone changes, except for me.

One at a time I study the notices. I could have been more. I am too thin, too insubstantial. I could have been more. I am expiring.

'Lal,' says Peggy O'Farrel, she's at my shoulder.

'Lal,' she says again, but I'm not listening. I'm slipping from her noose, I'm unpinning a notice from the board. I'm saying to her, 'Would you happen to have some change, I need forty cents,' and then I'm heading out to the club foyer, past the drinkers and the pool players, to the public telephone.

I pick up the orange handset, it's thick and heavy. Peggy O'Farrel treads water at the carpet line between the foyer and the bar. The money drops, a man answers, soothing and confident, his voice licks deep into my ear, 'Bim Audette speaking.'

I make my call, because it suddenly occurred to me that, like a polar bear, I need both camouflage and breathing space, and there's no better place to hide than in the open.

CHAPTER THREE
A DAY AT THE BEACH

It's the next day and it's hot, and Davey and I are going down to the beach. I'm rummaging around the fridge for a few treats to make the packed lunch more festive, because there's a sort of holiday atmosphere in the air. There's been a cool spell like you think maybe autumn wants to stay but this weekend's shot back to stinking hot and you want to hang onto it, the last late-March blast of summer. Davey's chucked his big black flippers into the tray of the ute and he's just about to heave the beach umbrella in like a striped torpedo when I yell out, 'Be careful with that thing, it's getting old.' He does everything so roughly. And then it's always the thing's fault when the thing gets broken. 'Bloody stupid plate,' he says, when he breaks one washing up, whacking it on the tap on the way up from the suds to the drainer. It makes me wonder how he hasn't fried himself at work. He's a linesman with the County Council and I shudder to think of him so clumsy and buggerising about with the precise and deadly zing of electricity.

The contents of the fridge aren't that inspiring but there's a tin of ham and a packet of camembert cheese to add to the bread rolls out of the freezer, plus the half a carrot cake

I pinched from work awhile back. Of course, there're also a zillion mandarins. I dig into one now and the whole sharp sweet smell of it fizzes and falls out in a circle with its peel. Last week Davey came in all pleased with a six-kilo bag of them from the single mother who runs the fruit and vegie hut on the Coolie back road.

'First of the season,' he'd said. 'She reckons they're from Porter's place.'

'Very nice,' I'd said, 'but you didn't need to buy that many.'

'No, I didn't need to buy that many,' he said, 'but, Lal, she sits in that rough shed all day, only the occasional passer-by – it seemed to me she needed to *sell* that many. We can give them away.'

He's a softie, does these small generous things far more often than I do, will lend whatever strength he has to anyone weak. There, I'm going all drippy on him but not for long. I throw away the mandarin skin and glance up through the back door in time to see an aluminium deck-chair somersault through the air and land with a crash over the tailgate into the ute.

I make my way down the hall to the linen press and swing open the double doors. There's the spotted beach bag and into it I put the towels and an old picnic rug, its tiger stripes worn thin. There's the plastic pillow from the BP service station which Davey likes to snooze on and the little toilet bag into which I'll put a wet flannel so we can wipe our hands. Funny how you do the things your mother did even when they use to drive you crazy. As a kid I'd hop up and down the hall in my swimming togs, impatient to be gone and Mum would be mucking round in the bathroom wetting the flannel. 'Come on, Mum.' I'd hop from one floral cluster on the carpet to another, trying not to wobble off balance and fall down into the gold background colour. When I came down extra hard the glass in the china cabinet would rattle. 'Will you stop that thumping,' she'd call. There was only bathroom echo in her voice, no anger or threat of it. She just said it because she was a mother and she had to. She didn't even like the china cabinet. She just owned it because she had to.

'Come on, Mum.'

I look up from the tap to the mirror and there's my big face, but for an instant I think it's someone else's. I look straight into my eyes to pin the reflection back onto me. Behind my head, in the mirror, I see through the open door into the bedroom and notice the curtain has dropped off its track in one place and is hanging in an ugly little loop. I don't know how long it's been like that. I might have walked past it fifty times without noticing it before now.

The curtains are a lovely tealy kind of aqua blue and the bedspread is purple and green. My neighbour, Viv, was with me when I bought that bedspread.

'You must be crazy,' she'd squawked.

She said it so loudly that the other women in the shop turned their heads to check my sanity for themselves.

'It'll never go.'

I held it up. Sealed in its thick clear-plastic cover, it was heavy.

'Just because it's on sale doesn't mean you have to take it regardless of taste.'

Some of the shoppers who had swivelled their necks to see, pulled faces in agreement with Viv.

'You don't see those colours in nature.'

'Viv, you don't know anything about nature.' I put the bedspread down on top of some others and smoothed out a crinkle in the plastic.

'Lal, the natural look is in as a decorating device, so believe me, I know about nature. I've read about it.'

'I've seen these colours together in rock pools.'

'Rock pools!' she snorted with disgust, then slammed down a brown geometric.

At the counter the lady took my money and then patiently squeezed and eased the bedspread into a carry bag which was too small for it. She smiled as she handed it over.

'They're such a bargain,' she said, 'you can't be too fussy.'

When I got it home Davey said, 'I don't want to lie in all those flowers. All that purple and green.'

'Oh, my poor little elf.'

'Fairy. I'll turn into a bloody fairy,' he'd said. 'You've made it into a girl's bedroom and I don't feel like I belong.'

I yanked on the cord to part the curtains and they swished at the bottom like opening night at some posh theatre. Spread out was the sun-sharpened back yard, a big patch of buffalo grass and, centre stage, a broken car engine.

'There,' I'd said to him, 'does that make you feel better?'

That was two years ago, and while the bedspread has stayed, the engine has thankfully been removed. With the curtains shut against the strong sunlight as they are today, the white walls take on a blue tinge. So the room does have the look of a sea pool. Today it's a pool in a coral reef because it's cool and warm at the same time.

I'm standing on a chair trying to work the hooks back into the binding on the curtain when I hear Davey's china cabinet-rattling footsteps up the hall.

'Come on, Lal. Are you ready yet? Car's packed.'

His big body fills up the doorway and he says, 'Jesus. What are you doing now?' And then he whistles, 'Just look at those legs!'

I've just got my togs on with a T-shirt over the top. I hope he doesn't mind too much about the tiny broken capillaries which have started to scribble themselves in places under the surface of my skin. At thirty-eight years old, forty is approaching fast and I'm sensitive to these things. Callused shop girl feet, crazed capillaries, settling weight – ageing is a great unfairness. I'm not fully formed yet, haven't done enough with either my body or my brain, but here I am, already bearing witness to the slow dismantling of the incomplete person who is me.

'Lal?' says Davey, he's seen my mood slip. He comes over and runs his hand appreciatively up one leg to my thigh and he smiles and says, 'You can still make me twitch.' I bat his hand away from my crotch, laughing, restored, 'Get out of there.' I jump off the chair and he's bustling me along down the hall, pinching my bum as he goes, calling out at the top of his voice like it's some silly battle cry, 'To the beach! To the beach!'

We get in the car for our four-minute drive. Davey turns the radio up high. We've got the windows wound right down, the air blowing in, we're singing the do-wops and I'm beginning to feel better than I have for days – ever since encountering the dentist's father. Last night at the club may yet have a positive outcome. It's time to try and move forward.

We pull up in the car park at the Surf Lifesaving Club, gravel crunching under the tyres and the aluminium deckchairs clattering over in the back. As it happens we've parked right next to Ray and Viv's brand-new saloon car so they're somewhere here too. We load up with as much stuff as we can carry and when we stagger to the end of the boarded track through the low dunes it's all worth it. The beach is polka dotted with umbrellas between the limp flags. Too lazy to work up a regular rhythm, the waves fall and hiss, green where they curl and break, but further out where they first gather themselves up they're eye-blue. The headland bakes itself older in the already hot sun.

'It's rare,' says Davey appreciatively.

He's not a regular beachgoer – he seems to forget it's there or forget what it's there for, concentrating as he does in his leisure time on murdering fish. But like today, when he does come, he loves it.

'You two relocating the local tip?' murmurs Viv when we find her and dump all our stuff beside her.

'Where's Ray?' asks Davey.

Viv nods towards the water and sinks back onto her gorgeous towel. Davey takes himself off.

Lying back propped on my elbows I watch the swimmers bob and disappear into rolls of foam, the boogie board riders curve and skim. You don't get many days as perfect as this. Out the back the orange lifesaver's rubber ducky patrols the swell, its engine audible now and then when it's on an up-rise. The beach is sometimes subject to dangerous rips so we cluster up this end where the flags tell us to, but the proper surfies ride at intervals all along and even right up to the point with its wedding-cake shelves of foaming reef. It's a great view but I'm glad we live on the inlet, on the bay side of Pocket Head. We still get salty airs (as well as the smell of cut grass and dog shit) but we're not blasted by the wind like the houses here and up at the Heights on the cliff line.

'Viv,' I say, 'when the Audettes moved here, did you sell them their block of land?'

'Yeah,' she monotones.

She's in real estate. She's also in some half-cooked hypnotic trance and, like a stroke victim, can only talk out of the corner of her mouth.

I'm looking up at the Audette house now, it's the biggest one in the string along the clifftop, all angles and stark, like a glass eagle's nest or a control tower to regulate the weather and the waves.

'What're they like?'

'Rich.'

I press her for something more but all she can muster is a half sentence, 'Argued among themselves, but they weren't a challenge.'

I natter on about other inconsequential things and I'm really talking to myself, Viv's drifted off again, but when I tell her I've just joined the Historical Society she wakes up with a start.

'Good heavens! Whatever for?'

Davey comes panting up the sand spluttering sea water and runny snot, 'Come on, Lal, s'beautiful in.' He starts searching for his flippers.

'Davey,' says Viv tucking her ash-blonde hair behind her ears, 'do you know what your wife's been up to?'

I love the shock of the first surge of cold water when it comes over your pubic bone and makes you suck in your stomach muscles with a gasp. When it nips at your waist you dive into the comb of the first unavoidable, oncoming wave. In that moment of burble under the sea the roots of your hair spring to attention with cool relief. It's like you've unzipped one layer of dirty puffy skin and stepped out wearing a firm fresh one. Due to the water pressure, you've gone down a dress size and taken off twenty years. Suddenly you're an alpine maid with enough energy to yodel across great valleys of crisp mountain air.

Viv said she thinks the Historical Society will be full of old women and dickheads.

I tried to tell her it couldn't be, the president is Bim Audette, he's a man of high standing and wouldn't waste his time on anything inconsequential.

Viv said he had vested interests.

I suppose she means because he's the grandson of Girlie Tyler, Pocket Head's only hero.

I tried to bring Viv round, I told her that, though I'd never spoken to him before, he was welcoming over the phone. He was sincere and reassuring. His voice was burgundy and deep, and, despite the tin-pot din of the club, you'd never have known there were a couple of miles of impersonal wire connecting up his words to my ear.

Viv was deadpan, 'He's not the Messiah.' She turned over to bake her other side. 'He's an ageing ex-football star, born and bred in Coolie. And even if he did escape for a while, since when did anything good ever come out of Coolie?'

I'm trying to get out past the breakers but I'm kept busy for a bit while a big set of waves roll in, each one sucking away the water before it with a prodigious thirst and then pounding it back down, like a drinker draining a glass and slamming it onto the bar. A couple of kids get caught unawares, bowled over, and their brightly coloured boards corkscrew out of the boiling foam like brief modern sculpture. Davey, I see, is at hand to set one little girl to rights, he puts her back on her feet and holds her board while she wipes her sandy plait from her face. She's a little shaken but laughs when he swims away making a fin with his hand and pretending, quite successfully, given his body shape, to look like a great white shark.

We borrowed a child once. Just for a little while. It was lovely. He was Ray and Viv's boy, Tony. He's fourteen years old now and away at boarding school but when we borrowed him he was only six.

Ray had won a trip for two to Honolulu in a shaving cream competition so Tony stayed with us for a week. It was like we'd gone on holidays too. We went swimming. Davey let him ride round town in the back of the ute and watched cartoons with him. I took him fishing off the jetty with Dad. Dad taught him how to clean and gut a fish and Tony poked into its insides, asking which was the bit that made it float.

That fish got pretty mangled, and by the end of the lesson Tony had scales in his hair and bright specks of gore on his thin arms. I put him in a bath when we got home and had to scrub hard at the dried-on blood. His skin still had the pearly softness of a baby's. My hands holding the flannel and soap looked too rough to touch him.

I couldn't sleep that night for worry. Davey lay awake too, with all my tossing.

'What if something happened to him while he was in our care?' I whispered.

'Nothing will happen.'

'But he's such a little boy, he's really still a baby. Bad things can happen. Anytime. He could be asleep in there and forget to breathe.'

When I woke up the next morning Davey was not in the bed. Muffled giggles came from Tony's room. I opened the door to see Tony leaping off the bed onto a camp mattress on the floor. Davey was about to attack with a pillow.

'Aunty Lal, Uncle Dave was here! He stayed the night,' said Tony. He was beaming with his good luck.

'Yeah, well,' said Davey, 'I was just making sure.'

Two weeks after the holiday when I was ironing, doing some of the things you leave in there at the bottom of the basket until next time, there was a pair of Tony's shorts. They looked so tiny next to Davey's humungous King Gees. I smoothed them out. I pulled at the pockets to iron them flat but there was a dull lump in one. It was sand. Half a handful, a child's half handful of sand. Davey walked by, saw me staring, and came over. It made a lovely little dune tipped out onto the board. How had it survived the washing machine and flapping on the clothes line to be discovered now, a long way from the beach? We couldn't seem to take our eyes off it.

'It doesn't matter,' said Davey.

The unbroken waves lift me gently, hold me briefly on their crests the way a father holds up a child for a better view, and then, arms tired, they subside. Up and gently down. Lift and float.

I let the sea use me more kindly these days. The winter after Mum left I went swimming every day while I waited for her return. I wanted my body to feel number than my brain. I sought out the coldest currents, daring them to cramp me, and flirted with their drag. When I could swim no more I stood ankle deep in the shallows, letting the wind graze my skin blue and hook up goosebumps. I stared over the wide ocean, some days wishing fancifully for a cargo boat to come chugging over the horizon with Mum waving from the railing, 'See, Lallie, I told you I'd come home.'

She never did.

I went, cold and dripping, back to Dad. He wasn't much help. He had become a different father, a sorrow-struck man, silent and curled up within himself. *Your father watched.*

The dentist's *National Geographic* magazine said it's common practice for Eskimo mothers to give away their babies. I don't understand it. No regrets or backward glances. Those Eskimo mothers pass their swaddled parcels to sisters or cousins or friends, whoever has the greater need. I know the need for a child *and* I know what it's like to be abandoned. So either way, I don't understand it.

Davey's face plips up from under the water and he bobs beside me. His brown hair is plastered flat and straight on his head with just the pink tips of his ears poking out. He looks like a seal, you know how they have those little knobs for ears on the sides of their heads. He blinks the water from his eyes without bothering to wipe it away.

'I didn't know you were interested in history,' he says.

I shrug as best as I can while keeping afloat.

Hope he's put suncream on those ears.

'Why didn't you tell me?' he says.

I tell him it's not important, just swim, but he seems to want to make something of it.

He says, 'What do they do, the Historical Society?'

I'm cross with myself because I don't know what they do, but I'm hanging onto the sound of Bim Audette's firm voice and how it somehow held a promise.

Davey tells me the Lions Club lets in women members now and I could be a Lioness instead, but I tell him flatly no thanks, I'm not interested.

'It's crap, Lal, this society,' he spits out sea water. 'Who gives a shit, who cares about the past?'

'I do,' I snap. 'Maybe I'll go along there and I'll find out something I don't know and I'll like knowing it. That's an achievement. That could be something useful to me.'

He can't think of anything to say quick enough and that makes him cranky so he shakes his seal head at me and performs a neat duck dive. He's much more graceful in water than on land, except that as he curves over to disappear underwater his Speedos don't quite cover his big bottom and he shows off a fair bit of crack.

The sand's hot. Even with the insulation of a wet layer of it caked onto your feet it's boiling hot and you have to dance in under the umbrella for a bit of shade so you can stand still long enough to get yourself organised, dry yourself, find your sunglasses. Sand was never this hot when we were kids.

Viv's basting herself with coconut oil and Ray's offering to do her cleavage. I tell them to help themselves to whatever's in our esky, I'm walking to the point. After my disagreement with Davey I've lost my appetite. Ray opens the lid of the esky and peers in, 'What's with all the mandarins?'

I plant my feet, one after the other, along the water's edge, just where the wash peters out in semicircular licks as it polishes the sand and leaves a residue of white bubbles.

I've always been a walker, especially when I get ruffled or upset. Mum was a walker too. Dad was a man for a chair.

When Mum walked she'd pick flowers from gardens and smoky-blue leaves from the bush and come home with them tucked into buttonholes or peeking from the cloth band of her hat. Personal souvenirs from a trip abroad. 'You look lovely,' Dad would say, and with studied precision he'd pick the blooms off her, one by one, like an expert defusing a bomb. As if to show off his skill and to celebrate her return, he'd put her private pickings into a glass on the windowsill, on display. She, somehow diminished, would look away.

I miss the glad sight of her wearing those tiny bouquets.

At the point I pick my way over the rock shelf, over the sandstone faults and folds, where you can see the way the world boiled the day before it cooled. I dodge little holes, brackish with the sick mixture of rainwater and old sea, stepping closer to the spray and the sloosh of the waves until I find a good deep pool, a perfect trapped garden. There's nothing like a rock pool to turn you peaceful. I fill my gaze with speckled anemones, red and green, with the brilliance of a shred of sea lettuce, with walls studded with the licorice and striped humbug of countless periwinkles, with the pentagon of a slate-grey sea-star and another brushed with a shy tint of pink.

Beautiful.

Some little bug or fish, it's too quick to tell which, flits behind a rock, a ghost fish, you can see right through it.

I've got to know a few of the names and some of the

strange habits of creatures living in the tidal zone since I found a book a few months ago called *Wonders of Australia's Shores and Seas*. It was lying round at Dad's and I thought it was his, but when I opened up the cover there was Mum's handwriting. Though I don't recall ever seeing her read it, the way her name is written in such confident biro-blue makes it seem as if the book was important to her. I took it and didn't tell Dad. It's pretty old but it has some lovely photographs. Wish they were in colour. It doesn't really matter, I can use my memory and imagination and paint them as I like. That book has become as necessary to my night-time comfort as a pillow. I read a paragraph or two before I put out the light and in the dark I think of all those creatures going about their business under the chipped skull of the moon.

If I could be young again I'd get myself some scuba lessons and buy some equipment and set off under the waves to see that strange world for myself. Davey would be horrified. But if I'd had a pastime like observing underwater life I wouldn't have to have joined the Historical Society. I could have studied something, watched a small creature and made notes and measurements. It could have been useful. There must be some things that real scientists would quite like to know except they're too busy. I could study blennies or gobies, I like the sound of them, they're little fish; or anemones – or even giant kelp.

When I open up my seaside book at bedtime it irritates Davey. He says stuff like, 'Why don't you get yourself a story, something interesting to read.'

He likes ones about Nazi hunters and the Cold War and double-crossing spies.

'This *is* interesting,' I say and I try to tell him titbits which would surely fascinate an amateur fisherman. He burns round in boats on top of the sea but he wouldn't have a clue about what's going on underneath. For him, the fish he plucks up just materialise out of the void, it's like being blind and sticking your arm in the fish shop window.

'That's boring shit,' he says before I have a chance to read out loud, 'I don't know how you stand it.'

I suppose when I'm mad and old like the dentist's father I'll be spouting out this seaside stuff, still trying to find someone to listen. To each his own, that's okay, but sometimes your own gets lonely.

The tide's rising. A seventh wave breaks and trills over the rock platform and I step back to drier strata.

Maybe I didn't do a very good job of explaining to Davey about the Historical Society just now, but I'm not just joining to hide behind its facade. I'm sick of staying the same. Information can help you change your opinions and ideas.

For instance, before I read the jellyfish chapter in my book, I used to regard bluebottles as nasty bastard things that interfered with your swimming and ought to be killed for it. When they blow in in bulk you can't take to the water because their long stingers'll burn you like hot needles if they brush against you. But now I've read about them I'm fascinated. For example – and it's hard to believe – did you know that a bluebottle is not one animal but a floating colony of joined but different individuals which function as a whole? Bizarre. It's a little floating town.

Other types of jellyfish are interesting for other reasons. Like those jellies that softly headbutt their way round the inlet. Scientifically they're something unpronounceable but we call them man-o'-wars. They're not beautiful, they're big ugly blubbers, brown-domed and with eight white horrible thick legs which look like spinach gone to seed. We used to bomb them with rocks when we were kids. Not beautiful to look at – until now when you're grown up and can stand still long enough to watch them move. Spaceships in water. Umbrella spasm, silent glide. Sometimes they appear in hundreds, even millions maybe, all propelling the same way, the inlet thick with layers of them, like a lush underfelt for the sleek surface of water. My book doesn't say why man-o'-wars sometimes mass but marvels at the numbers – so many they can even be seen from an aircraft one thousand feet in the air. I give up fishing now when they swarm that dense, it's too hard to avoid hurting them with hook and line, and I worry about the gnat-like boats churning through them chopping them up with propeller blades. It might be my fancy, but the old oysterman, who's always skulking about, doesn't use his outboard motor much, prefers to row – sensitive, I imagine, to doing damage. I've watched him bend his back in the distance and pictured his oars dipping, brushing the jelly-blubber domes. The touch of the blades, stroke-gentle.

The oysterman is such a constant, silent presence on the inlet that sometimes it seems as if he's a natural phenomenon himself.

He was there the night something very special happened. It was when I was about fourteen. I met Mum coming back from her evening walk and her face was flushed and her dress was damp up to her waist. 'Come and look,' she said and she dragged me by the hand to the foreshore. Tiny shore waves trimmed the bay with a continuous fizz of sequinned light. It was phosphorescence.

I waded in up to my knees and kicked up a splash. Showers of light. Fireworks sparks. The wonder of it. We threw rocks into the deep and watched them drop with glowing trails of seltzer. Fish in the shallows scooted in neon dashes. When we looked up into the greater dark of the inlet there was the oysterman rowing by in his boat and headed for home. His oars dipped in the inky black making molten circles of gold.

'I think he did it,' said Mum.

Molten ripples.

I thought so too.

But, as mysterious as he sometimes seems, it wasn't him and it was a bit of a disappointment to have that magical possibility removed. According to my book, marine phosphorescence like we saw that night is caused by tiny creatures and the light happens when a chemical which they contain is excited by movement. Would I have waltzed in the water if I knew my legs were crawling with bugs?

Davey would say that proves there are some things you don't need to know. But how do you know what you need to know without knowing it? A seagull squawks close overhead, it's hovering wing-stretched but tilting drunk in an uplift of the breeze, poised to steal anything worthwhile that I might have disturbed. Disappointed when nothing's forthcoming, it rips off to harass a rock fisherman hacking at cunjevoi down near the wash of the surf.

I'm wondering if Davey and Ray and Viv have left me anything to eat.

CHAPTER FOUR

FISHING FOR HISTORY

It takes them forever to leave. In and out of the house and the garage fifty times. Next thing you know your best knife's been swiped out of the kitchen drawer and is disappearing out the back door. Doesn't matter how many fishing knives Davey's been given as Christmas presents over the years.

Coor*whit*. Crash. There goes the screen door again and I bet when they've left I'll go to shut it properly and it'll be jammed half off its runner. I can hear some bloke in the laundry rummaging in my deep freeze. About now he'll be pulling out the baskets and balancing the ice-cream and the meat on the washing machine and any minute, yep, there it is, a chicken or a leg of lamb skates off and hits the lino. It's always a thinner sound than you're expecting. There's no swearing, so it didn't get him on the foot this time. There's always next weekend.

Now there's a satisfied 'Ah ha' as he hits paydirt – he's located the bait collection – and then you can hear everything else getting dumped back in. I had a homemade ginger-fluff sponge cake in there but now it's probably a bag of bits. Outside there's the thud of car doors slamming,

Davey's calling out orders about backing up the ute and someone's tipping ice into one of those foam eskies. Davey calls the esky their lifeboat.

'Get us a rag, you prick,' is the next song drifting in through the window, followed by 'coor*whit*', and there's Col standing in front of me saying, 'Lal, we need a rag, he's spilt fish oil.'

Col is the most sheepish member of the Old Boys Network, as they like to call themselves, and is sent on purpose, because then they know I can't get cross with him.

When that polished fibreglass monster of a boat finally trails majestically out of the driveway behind the ute I could almost cheer. But I don't. I sit at the kitchen table a bit longer. In case they've forgotten something.

The boat is Davey's pride and obsession. It's an 18ft Haynes Hunter with a 90hp Mercury, an echo sounder and a cabin you can barely sit in. The engine costs us a fortune in maintenance and fuel bills before we've even made a payment on the thing. Scrawled across the hull in orange running writing is its name – *Extractor*.

Blithe – breezy, confident, foolish word – that's how they are, those boys in their boat, and I get nervous for them. I wish they'd fish the inlet but they peel out through its mouth to plunge into ocean swells; the *Extractor*, ark-like inside our garage, shrinks to a dot on the lip of a big horizon. Confidence begging trouble. I have to worry, it's my job to worry, because it's an insurance policy. You can help protect yourself and others if you worry the right way. Bad things always take you by surprise. They wait until your back is turned and just when you relax and think you're walking safe they jump out at you from behind a lamppost. That's what happened when Mum disappeared. But if you're alert and learn to sometimes walk backwards you can avoid a lot of trouble, at least for a while or until something falls onto your head because you never thought to look up at the sky. Okay, the theory has its flaws but I'm scared of everyone disappearing or dying and leaving me alone, so surely it's better to try and worry away some trouble than be vulnerable to it all. How can I not worry about Davey when they could take a wave, get struck by lightning, sink without a trace? Far better seafarers than Davey have met their end in these dangerous waters. The treachery of this coast is such that one of the first lighthouses in New South Wales was built on the headland here. It was built by convicts, and that's how Pocket Head got its name – after the pickpockets and petty thieves who camped here.

These days they've got a navigation light on top of Middle Skittle, the highest pillar in a clump of rocks three miles out to sea, so the Pocket lighthouse isn't in use anymore. It has a bit of a dark history anyhow. One night in 1917 the keeper on duty got drunk and let the light go out. Which was just as well, some might say, because it's the only dramatic thing that's ever happened in Pocket Head.

The lighthouse keeper had rotten luck. At least, that's what I reckon. So Senior Keeper Wilson had a few drinks. Can you blame him? It would have been pretty lonely sitting up there at the top of that spiral staircase looking out to sea. If you're standing next to that big lamp and it's blinking on-off, on-off, your eyesight could need some soothing. Anyway, you have a few drinks and then you're nodding. Actually, you must have got pretty sloshed if you can sleep with that light going on and off. Meanwhile the junior keeper is snoring in his bunk in the cottage because he shared a few tots with you before turning in.

The light goes out.

The headland is dark.

The weather worsens.

The weather is dire.

The steamship *Angel* comes clawing up the coast.

Her cargo shifts.

You stir too, your dreams disjointed by drink. Big breasts. Laughter. Mummy crying. Music hall songs. A slab of bread dripping with syrup.

The *Angel* pitches. A wall of water. Her boilers flooded.

You turn over and sink, sink, back to sleep.

The *Angel* grinds on reef.

You disappear completely into the black plum of sleep.

In the dark, sixteen lives are lost and only one is found.

They say Senior Keeper Wilson was generally a sober man, but he got all the blame.

The cargo shifted.

It seems unfair.

He might have picked a hundred other lonely nights to drink. The *Angel* would have gone down light or no.

But rescue would have come sooner.

As it was, nobody knew until dawn.

The *Angel* turned out to be a money-spinner, though, and it literally put Pocket on the map. Before then, Coolie was the only cartographers' dot. Photographers from Sydney and Newcastle rushed to take pictures of the *Angel*'s broken shape, which was easily visible from the beach. Tragedy's quite an attraction. People came from miles around to rubberneck, some on organised tours, dressed in their Sunday best for the occasion; picnics and parasols. The only survivor, Girlie Tyler, became a hero. She was downright famous. Still is. 'The Flower of the Storm', the newspapers called her. Somehow it captured the imagination of the day – the delicacy of a woman denying the brute appetite of an uncontrollable sea.

It's all old news now, yet we're hammered with it. I've seen all those photographs a hundred times; the local newspaper, the *Angel Advertiser*, reprints them at the drop of a hat and they pop up framed on office walls and behind pub bars and in municipal halls all over Coolie. In fact, Coolie has rather hijacked the tragedy. Girlie Tyler's white stone statue looms over passing cars from the middle of a traffic island at the meeting of Coolie's three main roads. Girlie and the *Angel* have become emblems for the whole shire, which rather peeves Pocket Headers.

On the seventy-fifth anniversary of the wreck they held a memorial service down at the beach, though, of course, there was nothing left of the *Angel* to pray by since the last of it broke up in a gale in 1925. Davey and I went along to watch the fuss but we didn't last long. Too many dignitaries spouting out too many boring speeches. And you couldn't hear them properly even if you'd wanted to because the wind muffled the PA system. We went home.

Now I think of it, I suppose the Historical Society would have been involved in an event like that. That's not what I want to get involved in, not official stuff like that. The grinning spectre of Davey looms and it's jeering, 'I told you so.'

It's a disturbing image. Luckily, it catapults away when a

do-your-washing kind of wind comes gusting through the window, threatening to wrench the net curtain right off its rod. The almost-empty bottle of dishwashing liquid wobbles on the sill and then commits suicide into the sink, oozing green blood. Bills and junk mail scatter over the lino, you could kick through them like dead leaves. I hope those boys don't go out too far today. I survey the damage they've left behind and decide on the unfortunate necessity of a thorough clean. I do housework begrudgingly, can't find anything good about it, whereas Mum always turned it into a game. She'd turn the record player up loud, Barbra Streisand and Tom Jones, and do small dance steps behind the vacuum cleaner. She scrubbed the bath in time to Broadway hit tunes and, for a little while, our house would seem as bright and airy as the USA.

As I lurch up from the kitchen chair to begin my assault, I slip in Col's fish oil footprint. The agenda's set. Floors first.

It takes me until well after lunch to finish my work and, as a reward, I decide I'll pop down to the jetty and go fishing myself. Davey won't bring home much, if any, since the Old Boys Network only goes after the big stuff which they sell on the sly. In my opinion little fish are sweeter eating anyway, their tails curl and crisp in the pan.

I go and ring up Dad and ask him if he wants to come but he says it's a Sunday and he never fishes on Sundays. I tell him we often fish on Sundays but he says he's been checking through his diary and for the last eight weeks he's mowed the lawn on Sunday, so that's a routine now and can't be broken. I sigh into the phone and he reprimands me for getting huffy. I'm starting to hate those diaries, I'd like to chuck them away. He always was a person who preferred things to stay the same, even to the point of getting Mum to cook the same food on the same day each week. She hated the tedium of a set menu but he insisted it was better that way because then you knew what to look forward to. I might be overly suspicious, but gradually over time Dad's set of routines has been getting ever more extreme and rigid.

'It's lawn day today,' he says, 'not fish day.'

'Yes, Dad,' I say.

I head over to the garage to get my gear. That's another thing I hate – the garage. It's just a great big stone round our necks gathering the moss of debt. Davey is oblivious to the financial crisis it's caused and can only think what a good idea it was to build a garage double the size of any owned by his mates. I protested against the whole idea at first but quickly gave in when he declared he'd cut costs and build it himself. I couldn't have that. Not after the letterbox.

We have the ugliest letterbox in the street. If it were that little bit bigger we could use it as a bomb shelter. Or I could turn it into one of those end-of-the-world pantries. What religion is it where they have to last out for so many days until God rescues them? It's hard to believe but true – our letterbox could effectively store a bulk supply of canned soup and smoked hams.

I'd wanted to duck into K-Mart to get a replacement after the old letterbox rotted off the post. But oh no. Davey said, 'I'll make a new one.' It didn't seem like a good idea to me, having seen the billycart he'd once made for Tony, our boy next door. It sure was a wobbly-looking jalopy, but not for long. The design failed to include a brake.

'It's just a letterbox,' Davey insisted, 'I'll make one.'

The next weekend, I went with Viv to Sydney to see the new production of *Cats,* and when we got back it was done. The postman has since complained about grazing his hand.

When we pulled into the driveway Davey was sort of hopping from side to side on his big yellow-thonged feet, impatient for us to get out of the car so he could take us on a tour of his construction.

'My dear,' said Viv.

'Did the boys come round to help you with the foundations?' I said.

He looked a bit cross and replied petulantly, 'No, I made it all myself.'

'Were you drunk?' asked Viv.

The letterbox stands about four feet high and has a girth of volcanic proportions. It is a great glumping mound of grey knobbly concrete, stuck all over with seashells.

'It's my Taj Mahal to you, Lal,' said Davey tenderly.

'Are you going to bury me in it?' I asked.

He was too busy to hear, producing a pretend letter out of his shorts pocket and demonstrating posting methods through the gaping maw at the front. Then he skipped round the back to show us the ease of retrieval. He fumbled with the latch on a white-painted door which was, in itself, big enough to admit a large dog.

'It'll loosen up with use,' said Davey, referring to the latch.

And then he got it free and opened the door in a wide arc, a smile breaking over his face. What we were now looking at was a great, cavernous black hole.

'Plenty of room at Christmas time,' said Davey. 'And if they ever start delivering milk again it'll stay beaut and cool.'

As we turned to the house he whispered quietly, so Viv couldn't hear, 'I ran out of shells for the inside, but I don't think it matters if there's none on the inside.'

'No,' I whispered back, 'it doesn't matter.'

That night we urged Viv to get Ray over and stay for a barbeque. We dragged our deckchairs round to the front porch and arranged them so that we sat like an audience beholding our monumental letterbox. Ray, balancing on a pot plant and the hand railing, reached up to the fascia board and re-pointed the porta-flood so its full glare bounced off the white shells embedded in concrete.

'Amazing, Davey,' said Viv. 'Single-handedly, in one weekend, you've devalued every house in the street.' She looked at Ray. 'We've got to fast-track our move up to the Heights.'

It took me a very long time but eventually I got to like the letterbox. At first I used to pray daily for an earthquake. For a start, the postman's right; the concrete's kind of sharp and you can easily scrape your knuckles if you're not careful. Also, I have to squat right down on my haunches to get the letters out. Davey has had to leave a little torch just inside the door so I can check I've got everything. This innovation came after the phone was nearly cut off. There's no denying it, the letterbox is an eyesore, but, over time, my own attitude has softened. How could it not? A gift is a gift and Davey meant his with love. So what if other women get roses? I've got – a unique blob. (Just once, I wouldn't mind roses.)

However fond I've grown of the letterbox, the point is, one construction of this nature is clearly quite enough and the prospect of Davey let loose on a grand-scale project like building a garage was enough to make me feel instantly bilious. There was a TV show once about this nutty Spanish architect, a Mr Gaudi who created the weirdest buildings, including a church with a bunch of spires that looked like old melted candlesticks. I had visions of Señor Gaudi turning in his grave with jealousy over whatever Davey might conjure up. I put my foot down and demanded professionals – ones who would produce a nice, plain, garagey-looking garage.

When Davey first parked the *Extractor* inside it, the new garage seemed as spacious as a ballroom but it didn't take him long to fill it up with junk. Today, I have to pick my way past all manner of indispensable marine items like broken bait traps, and the life jackets they've forgotten to stow on board, in order to get to the small corner where my fishing gear is stored.

Walking down our street I start to hurry up a bit, juggling my bucket, my rod, and the tackle box, because the tide looks promising, my timing's good. Over the roofs of the houses along the Esplanade I can see the water's already slurped in thin and covered the sand flats. At the end of the street Question Mark Man is striding away and I'm glad I've missed him, though he never holds me up for long. It's just that when you meet him it can be a bit disconcerting. He has a long oval face, smooth as an egg and capped with the salt and pepper of a short crew cut. His eyebrows egg up his forehead too, permanently raised in query. He's trying to be pleasant, I think, and he'll say something like, 'The sky is blue today?' or, 'The wind is biting?' and then he'll wait for an answer. It makes you confused for a minute as if you should stop and check the colours or examine your arms for tooth marks. Sort of surprised that it's true you confirm, 'Yes,' and his lips will go up in an egg smile, no teeth. He'll give a tiny satisfied nod and go briskly on about his business.

Question Mark Man goes walking twice daily. He always takes a different route so he's liable to turn up any old place. He lopes along with seven league-sized steps that his dog's barely able to keep up with. Davey jests and says he's going to ring the RSPCA because he reckons by the time that dog gets home the poor bugger must fall into its basket rooted.

The dog looks pretty energetic today, it's wagging its tail as they cut through Donovan's vacant lot, and so far Question Mark Man hasn't taken too big a lead.

When I get to the jetty it's empty, which is the best way for it to be, then there's no one else's chatter to disturb me or the fish, and I get to claim the prime spot, spread out my gear.

Yellowtail makes good bait except the fresh flesh mashes where I'm trying to cut skin. The knife's blunt again. They're cannibals – fish.

It's lovely down here. Always is. The whole spread of the inlet is laid out before me. I can see to the bushy headland near the mouth of the bay and across the water to Merrengong where the houses and boatsheds and jetties are painted with the butter of afternoon light. To my right, there's the oysterman's mangrove-edged bay. He's in his boat now, anchored at the corner of his lease, and the blue sinew of the inlet twists off behind him on its way between the wooded hills to Coolie. There's plenty of action to watch: sailboarders nip between the banks and the channel markers, a trawler peels back a neat scroll of bow wave, bird-shitted cabin cruisers turn on their moorings. The flying-boat shape of a pelican glides in and makes a soft splash as it applies the brakes.

It does you good to get out for a fish. It makes you feel like you're doing something when you're really not doing anything much at all. It gives you a chance to think. I'm meant to attend my first meeting of the Historical Society next Tuesday, so that needs some considering.

I thread a tiny fillet of the yellowtail onto my hook. You should never put on too much bait, it's a big mistake – fish just nibble the edges and don't go for the chomp and swallow. Unlike me. Rushing in.

I cast out, the line flicks off the reel, catches sun.

The sinker whacks the water dull and disappears. I wind up slack.

If only I knew more about what they did, the Historical Society.

It's not as if Pocket Head's got much history and what there is everybody knows anyway. You get the official version drummed into you in primary school – the *Angel* and the Actons, over and over. The Acton family was the first to settle this area and our teachers always used them as a local excuse to go on and on about colonial stuff. Way back in the year dot, they were given a land grant of practically the whole district. They ended up building this big homestead at Five Wells, halfway between what is now Coolie and Pocket. There were natural springs there. But the house burnt down and in later years the land got sold to shonky developers for a housing estate which never took off. Now there's a bus stop and a handful of dead-end shops, and Audette's Auto Acre – Wrecking & Smash Repairs.

I've always reckoned they should change the name of Five Wells to Poisoned Wells. The Actons couldn't get on with the local Aborigines, didn't want blacks in their backyard, so they poisoned three of the wells, keeping two fenced off and fresh for themselves. The Aborigines left, had to walk far away from their home and go somewhere strange. Terrible to have to leave your home against your will and wander, rootless forever, in foreign lands. Never to return.

I said to Viv once that I was thinking about writing a letter to the council requesting the name change because we should aim for the truth about things. She laughed. She said they'd write back saying the placename was accurate because there were, in fact, five wells and not six or four. She said they'd want to know how I proposed convincing the local shopkeepers that business would be enhanced when linked to the word 'poison'. She said they'd ask if the building inspector had been round yet to make his final report on my new garage, because, if not, they'd gladly oblige by sending him ASAP. Viv winked one heavily mascara-ed eye, 'Yours sincerely, Wallace Acton, Mayor'.

Ah – there's a bite on my line. But I've missed it. Might come calling again. When there's a fish niggling at his line Dad always sings this song:

Come little fishy,
Come calling again,
The bait is your dinner,
The hook is your friend.

If you're using prawn for bait you can sing all you like – you don't get second chances. It gets stripped off at the first hit. Yellowtail stays on better.

You know, Viv is right to be cynical about history, but the thing that I think is potentially interesting about history is what the schoolteachers don't tell you. And that's what I want to find out. The ordinary stuff that hasn't been cleaned up. How come the people in official history all seem stately and robotic just because they had different manners and clothes? Official time removes their warts, uncrosses their eyes, bestows intellect – ignores dumb luck – gives them purpose, while we, in the present, blunder around so much we might be mistaken for different animals.

I don't buy it.

For instance, just suppose that noble Phillip Acton was really a goat. Who said you had to be fantastic just to settle a bit of land? Some wily old governor, maybe Hunter or Bligh, may have used generosity as a ploy to hide a nuisance. After all, a nuisance in a new colony need not be tolerated. Imagine Governor Bligh, smirking behind his slim hand, sending Acton away with a sack of flour, a rat trap, and a new wife, chosen from a line-up at Parramatta jail. Let the birds listen to his loose flapping jaw. Imagine him aboard his ship as it kicks into the inlet, a dandy city boy, puffing out nervous little hot farts into his breeches.

Suppose his wife, Charlotte, was never a good-stick pioneer but hated her husband, appalled that he should set her down on a thin-lipped beach jumping with sandflies, and praying for the early invention of calamine. He tries to appease her with the promise of a homestead and she thinks, 'Yes, and I shall have a room in it far away from you if I have to quarry the sandstone myself with only my fingernails.'

History is so hung up on being great it forgets the blemishes which make it true and human. All that gumpf about an Acton master plan for the building of the town of Coolie – I bet they just sat tight on their bums watching it grow by default. Callused labourers humping bricks, butchers stuffing pink sausages, bootmakers, merchants of ribbon and lace, it's those people – drawn by the quid they could earn – who built Coolie, and ensured the Actons' comfortable survival. Because they, the ordinary people, brought with them two important things – the devotion for a steeple and the thirst for an inn – and all else followed.

Don't think I've got it in for the Actons, they were probably quite okay, it's just that I think a lot of private things which we don't get to know have a bearing on public matters.

Say I knew for sure that Charlotte Acton hated her husband's guts, then I'd be even more interested in her gardening exploits. She discovered the Coolie district was a perfect place for the cultivation of citrus trees and, more interestingly, she's also supposed to have been responsible for the popularisation of the passionfruit, having sniffed out a small bag of them from a South American trading ship and set them growing. If I knew she had a motive for her horticultural obsession, then I could give her credit instead of thinking she'd just stolen it from a convict yardsman. I'd believe that she escaped from her servant-slippered halls and the incessant yap of her silly husband to find refuge in the dark loam of a garden and the promise of seeds. I would hope it made her happy to watch her vines booming in the hot New Holland sun, running wild over her garden wall, running wild as if on school holidays, with their zesty taste, their passion flower. Her own invention. Flamboyant rogues in a dull colony.

If I could get to understand *why* people did things, not just what they did, it would be worthwhile belonging to the Historical Society. Look at Girlie Tyler, only she had the spirit to survive that shipwreck. What's the inside story? What made her the way she was and gave her such a good strong heart?

Whoompah! A solid hit. The dull, definite, unimaginative hit of a flathead. Its bellows mouth has opened up in a dumb circle and shut down over my sneaky hook. Has to be a flathead – not much fight under the arch of the rod but it makes its way to me with a telltale seesaw. At the surface it shakes its head and gives one weighty kick of its tail, showing white underbelly. Ugly but delicious. Just wait until I put this fellow in the pan and watch Davey lick his lips.

I feel a little rush of excitement as I land the fish and then work it onto its back so I can grab hold of its gills. You've got to be careful when you take out the hook because flatties have got spikes on their heads that can get you with a bit of poison. Hurry. This could be it. The silly season. The all-too-brief, all-too-easy-to-miss magic time in the rise of the tide where everything under the water is on the bite, and the bigguns are on the move. Well, big by my standards.

More bait.

CHAPTER FIVE
THE LIGHTHOUSE

The dirt road through the bush to the headland is in a shocking condition. The road must have run liquid up here during the May rains and now it's ten parts holes to ten parts rock. We jounce along. The cabin of Owen Klyster's old Landcruiser truck rolls from side to side as he eases the vehicle in and up and out of the ruts. Janet Constable's up front with Owen, bracing herself against the dashboard, but the rest of us are squashed in the back. Shoulder wedged to shoulder we're the one animal, leaning now this way – whoah – and then that. Over one extreme bump Bertie gets airborne, does a half-pike, and ends up with his head in Gaynor Daley's lap. He breathes in her smell, I swear it, before he removes his face from her skirt. She reddens and shifts as he blinks an apology.

'Sit up straight, Bertie,' Janet tosses back. She must have seen him with the eyes in the back of her head, but her voice is so bump-rattled it loses its edge of command.

It's not easy to hear anyway, so the conversation during the trip hasn't been rich. Once in a while Alf Sugarloaf leans over to talk at my ear. I can smell his words better than I can hear them. He's a smoker and his volume's lost in an emphysemic wheeze. I'm really too busy hanging on to pay any attention to what he says, and I'm watching my ankles because the floor is scattered with tools. Rakes and mattocks and shovels and paint tins go rumbling, rolling to the tilt of the truck. I feel like one of those Scottish dancers picking out foot space between the weaving blades of swords.

We're on a mission. We are the Pocket Head Historical Society and we're on the move. I've been to two of the monthly meetings now and this is my first tour of duty, as Owen calls it. He's in the army reserve, so he's up with all that talk.

They're all quite nice, the other members, although I'll have to admit my heart sank when I walked into the first meeting. Viv's words came back to haunt me, 'Old women and dickheads', when I saw Janet Constable there with her bosom pal, Iris Marchant. They're both knocking on sixty and not much fun. Janet runs Iris and the pair of them run Iris's husband Bertie to the point where newcomers to town can't work out which one is actually married to him. They all live together in the one house. Davey reckons Janet would do the sex to Bertie while Iris wrote out a shopping list to give to him when he finished. I shouldn't have been surprised to see them there, they belong to most things, but I had to try to stave off a panic attack when Janet launched off with the introductions.

Bim Audette welcomed me and asked me to tell everyone what my history was. That was a shock. I didn't count on having to say anything straight off. I thought I was going to listen in a corner. I started to squirm.

'I'll think of something and tell you next time,' I mumbled.

Bim brushed his big paw-like hand over his nose. A boxer's wave. I think he was hiding a smile. It was alright for him to be so safe and smug – he's got the history market cornered in this town.

'Ewe were born here in Pocket,' piped up Janet in my stead, 'married here to a local boy and set up your home.'

Her voice was tuttish. Smarten up, it said. I didn't look at her. I wanted to say shut up, you don't know anything about me.

'Your father, also a native, remains in the district, and is much respected for his lifelong service to the community as the local representative of the gas company.'

Janet paused here for effect and took another breath, fuel for a full head of steam.

'Your mother ...'

I should have seen it coming. I jumped in.

'My history is ...'

The others looked expectantly. Janet levelled her gaze at me, how dare I interrupt.

'My history is ...'

A pause as horrible as a loose tooth dangling on a thread and Janet dying to wobble it.

'Is ...'

I felt like crying. I don't have a history. All I've got is a departure note.

Janet edged forward in her seat.

'Your history is your history,' said Bim, 'and I shouldn't have put you on the spot first thing. My apologies.'

I could have kissed his green eyes. I nodded back, dignified.

The lunch room on the lot of Audette's Auto Acre didn't

seem a promising place to meet when Bim gave me the address, but there's nowhere to meet at Pocket anymore since the white ants got to the community hall. Where was the romance of history? At least the lunchroom is big and airy and brand new. It overlooks the Auto Acre through glass sliding doors with those little white rings painted on them so you don't charge out and bust your head open. Beyond the white rings you can see the smash repairs shed, office and paint shop, and the wrecking yard. There isn't one dark corner, it's all floodlit and tidy. Even the car bodies are stacked neatly, as if they form some precious collection and are only occasionally shifted around in order to be better admired.

Inside, the room is pretty Spartan – shiny lino and a satin gloss on the fake wood panelling which lines the walls. There're two large tables and also the big green stretch of a ping-pong table with plenty of space round it. You can imagine the lunchtime noise in that hollow room, apprentices with their blue-black overalls rolled down to their waist, lunging in steel-capped boots for the fragile little ball, and roaring for victory as they bear down for the smash over the three-inch net. We were so quiet in it. And polite.

After I'd got over having my cage rattled by Janet Constable, and the others got on with the business of the meeting, I started to settle in and enjoy studying the mismatched people ranged round the table. I wondered at their motives for being there because the common interest of history didn't seem like the only drawcard. For example, Shona Roberts and Rhonda Meekle seemed to be more engrossed in their knitting than anything else and I wouldn't mind betting they come along to get some peace away from their families. And I reckon Dr Ranold, who was reading the minutes, attends because he's a man in constant search of an audience. When you visit him professionally he always gives you a lecture and I dread going for pap smears because then he talks on and on into your nether regions. I thought I'd have to wait to find out about Gaynor Daley. She was a messy splodge of tie-dyed colour between Mr Marshall's sober suit and Alf Sugarloaf's corduroy. The MacDonald sisters were there too. It gives you the creeps if you look at them for too long because their tight grey curled perms are like pictures of the human brain.

And what about Bim Audette? He sat at the head of the table, filling the plastic chair with his ex-footballer's body. Despite being a large man and in his early fifties, he'd hung onto his fitness, still had the litheness of a sportsman when he shifted his legs to accommodate the ginger cat that leapt up onto his lap. He had thinning sandy-coloured hair and sandy eyebrows which gave him an approachable, friendly look, and was dressed in a Polo shirt, expensive baggy shorts and a pair of boat shoes. He looked to be one of those warm-blooded men who never feel the cold. Bim stroked the cat's head firmly and it pinned back its ears, squirmed for more, until his freckled forefinger strayed and lingered, petting the sparse fur under its neck, sending it into some kind of ecstasy.

At suppertime, when we were all milling about drinking cups of tea, Bim told me the cat was called Christine. His little joke, he said – it was his wife's middle name. Christine was boss of all the cats hanging round the yard and Bim was the only human she'd go to.

I asked him about the yard, how come it was so neat and

tidy, anything I'd ever seen to do with cars was usually filthy and revolting. He said, 'You know how little boys always want to grow up and buy the best train set? Well this is it,' and he jerked his thumb to point out through the window at the workshops, 'except I'm a motor mechanic by trade. Not that I worked at it much because of my involvement with sport, but I love cars.'

The old ladies gathered round then as if they didn't like me taking all Bim's attention. He was patient and charming with them, not at all condescending, but nevertheless retained a sort of relaxed authority, the princeliness of a benefactor. The MacDonald sisters hovered at each flank and Iris Marchant kept trying to pass him cake. 'Can't have our leader fading away to nothing,' she said.

He clearly attracts old ladies as well as cats. And maybe me.

So that was the first meeting and now I find myself bumping along in Owen's Landcruiser on the way to a busy bee at the lighthouse. The Historical Society is turning out more action-packed than I'd banked on. We're going out to tidy up the place, even though, what with the rough road, it doesn't get too many visitors.

Janet's still rabbiting on in the front seat and she's turning her stiff neck as far as it will go and talking over her shoulder at us and then she turns back to Owen and Owen's beard opens up and replies. We're bouncing round in the back on the hard seat and we haven't got a hope of hearing so we take it in turns to attempt nods of agreement every time she talks to the back seat. It's my turn and I nod, nod, yes, and then Owen holds up his long, science teacher's fingers to wave no. I shake my head to get up to date with the negative.

Owen teaches biology and Indonesian at Coolie High

School. The epaulets on the shoulders of his safari shirt arch up when he adjusts the rear-view mirror looking for support from the dummies in the back.

Finally, with dusty banksias scraping at the vehicle windows, we turn a bend in the narrow track and then we're out into the open space of the lighthouse car park. Bim Audette's expensive four-wheel drive is already there. He's unloading a slasher and a lawnmower out of the back of it, and Iris, his only passenger, waves us in to park alongside.

We're hardly out of the truck and straightening our bodies when Iris snaffles Bertie and drapes her white cardigan over his arm. He looks like a maître d.

'Just look at that!' she says, flicking her wrist with disgust towards the lighthouse and, more particularly, the two-foot-high graffiti defacing its walls. She grubs through items in the bottom of her handbag until she finds a pen and then she hangs the bag off Bertie's shoulder so she's free to copy down evidence in her notebook.

'There,' she says, 'I've got the girl's name, but is the last digit in her phone number a seven or a one?' She peers at the lighthouse. 'I'm going to ring that girl's mother. You see if I don't. She should know what her daughter's up to.'

Bertie concentrates on a flannel flower sprouting from the gravel at his feet and keeps his eyes as far away as possible from the additional spray-can boasts, 'great', and 'cocksucker'.

It's a shame to see the damage done by vandals. You get used to their work round Pocket – the street signs are forever being wrenched round their poles, but it's a bit sad when they get way out here and go to all that trouble to make a beautiful place ugly. Apart from the lighthouse walls, the car park is littered with broken bottles and cans, and there's a big burnt patch on the grass outside the keeper's cottage where someone's lit up a bonfire. There's more work to do than we'd expected.

We are allocated jobs and the tools get dragged out of the truck. Bim's going to do lawnmowing and rubbish collection, Alf, Iris, Janet and Gaynor are on gardening, and Bertie and Owen will paint over the graffiti. I've been given a paintbrush too but they sit me down next to a pile of blackened stones at the bonfire site and tell me to redo them white. The stones are car-park markers. I'm a bit disappointed but I can't say I can blame them. They must all have seen my house and – more to the point – our letterbox. They probably think I'm responsible for the design. You don't let someone of my dubious taste loose on a heritage building.

I get myself comfortable and begin dabbing away at the sooty rocks and I get to thinking that even a snail, if it had a hand to paint, would decorate its shell. The desire to decorate is irresistible. But nothing is ever as easy as you think and even dressing up the car-park stones is proving more of a challenge than first envisaged. In order to do the underneaths and to avoid putting too many black fingermarks on them, I devise a system of balancing the stones on top of the posts which fence off the keeper's cottage. Bim looks up from his rubbish collecting and laughs. He reckons I've made a cannibal's garden of skulls on sticks.

Janet Constable doesn't find my creative solution quite so amusing. 'Silly,' she mutters, but I think she's just jealous of our clowning round. As Alf comes huffing around the corner of the cottage with a rake, Janet interrupts us by calling across us to him, 'Alf, what's this I'm digging up?'

Alf's the horticultural expert – you should see his front yard.

'That's geranium, Janet, and I wish you wouldn't.'

'I told her to,' says Gaynor.

'May I ask why?' asks Alf, taken aback.

An argument starts. It's a philosophical argument.

Gaynor thinks they should be putting in native plants to make the place look much as it would have done when the lighthouse was first built and Alf wants the garden preserved the way the last keeper had it.

'Gaynor's got a point,' says Owen.

'No, Alf's right, isn't he, Iris?' says Janet, and she whacks her hand trowel down on the uprooted geraniums as if that will be enough to reverse the damage.

Alf, looking for a big majority, puffs out, 'Bertie, what do you think?'

Bertie is whistling away at his work and he's got no intention of letting himself get dragged into the debate. He's putting in some careful brushstrokes near the red gloss of the lighthouse door. I make up some business about having to clean my hands and mizzle off, not wanting to risk an opinion either.

Through a thick screen of bushes I follow a rabbit track. See the clouds ahead. Tissue scraps tumbling and rolling, tearing apart and writhing off to join up with another lot only to shred again. I've forgotten to look at clouds. I forgot they move so fast. Constant motion. This sure is a gassy planet.

The track takes a sharp turn down to the edge of the cliff and opens out to a warm slab of rock which must be sat on.

You could get a mania for world domination up here if

you were that way inclined. Queen of all you survey. Convicts would feel unjailed. Bury me here. The wild nip of Little Pocket Beach; ocean swells bashing themselves on bald rock before they slip round to the inlet mouth for a second altercation with the sandbar which spreads its arm across from the Merrengong side; the sandy stretch of Big Pocket Surf Beach; and, further north, the infamous old Black Angel Cove. Dead ahead the tottering pillars of the Skittles rising out of the sea – like blocks of flats for birds. Your heart pumps red and big and glory-filled with the beauty of it. If only because of this beauty, I'll never understand how Mum could leave.

Big white gannets circle in the middle distance over a school of fish. Watch them stay up without flapping their wings. How do they do that? They glide and hang, glide and hang. Hang. And then they drill down into a Red Baron nosedive. Kerplunk, a fat boy's splash cancels their grace.

Knock and clatter of tin, like the sound of a bell on a Greek mountain goat. It comes from behind me down the rabbit track. Bim appears, dragging a sack of rubbish.

'I'm watching the birds,' I say.

'Magnificent, isn't it,' he says, filling his eyes up with the sea and the sky.

For a minute neither of us talks.

And then he laughs at a big gannet bellyflop.

And then he says, 'I had to come back.'

I don't quite follow him but then he goes on to say he got to hate Sydney, he needed to come home.

'But you grew up in Coolie, didn't you,' I say, 'not here.'

'I was born on that beach.' And as he raises his hand to

point past the reef to Black Angel Cove his wedding ring bumps out a heavy flash of gold.

I laugh. 'You could be a lighthouse, Bim. Your ring could warn ships.'

He shakes his hand trying to catch the light again but it doesn't work.

'It seems I'm no more reliable than that one,' and he nods his head back to indicate the Pocket lighthouse. He plonks himself down on the rock beside me.

'It must have been pretty uncomfortable getting born on a beach,' I say.

He laughs.

'I didn't mean it literally, more spiritually,' he says.

He smiles with pride but it's humbled by a hint of apology. 'My grandmother was Girlie Tyler.'

As if I didn't know.

It suddenly seems a bit strange that Bim is here, maintaining the lighthouse that nearly killed his grandmother.

'Do you blame Senior Keeper Wilson for what happened?' I ask him, a bit anxious, as if it's a recent tragedy, and I should be careful not to offend.

'No,' he says, frowning, and he looks out to sea. 'He's not to blame.'

I'm glad about that. It's nice when someone thinks the same as you.

Bim gets up and picks up his hessian sack and I suppose it's time we returned to work, can't leave the others to do it all. Winding back along the rabbit track the white column of the lighthouse seems like the leaning tower of Pisa, it looms at a whacky angle over us.

'There's such a romance about lighthouses,' I say to Bim.

'Pharos,' says he, looking up at it.

That's the ancient name for them he tells me. I like knowing that. See, Davey, I have learnt something.

As we get back to the car park Owen is putting my dressed-up stones back in place under Janet's supervision and Alf is trying to help but Janet shoos him off, she's worried about the effect of heavy lifting on his dickey heart and cigarette-holed lungs. Bim and I pick up more litter. He says the first lighthouse ever built was one of the Seven Wonders of the World. In Egypt. In Alexandria. A massive structure three hundred and fifty feet high, and they kept a fire at the top which could be seen thirty miles out to sea. I'm thinking I wouldn't like to be the one who had to carry all that wood upstairs.

'Built in 270 BC!' Bim is breathless and it's not just bending down to pick up papers that makes him so. Bim says Alexandria must have been a fantastic city to live in, and what about Tolemy, he must have been a brilliant man, mustn't he, what with starting the library and re-digging the Suez Canal?

Bim is talking about this Tolemy fellow like he's everyone's best friend. I nod back to him feeling a bit of a fraud for not letting on that Tolemy and I are not acquainted but I don't want to interrupt. I like hearing him talk. It's not some tedious monologue, he keeps feeding me more, in spoonfuls I can manage. It's like I'm watching a show but I'm getting to be in it too. I'm mesmerised. He makes me think I'd like to live in Alexandria.

I ask him, 'How did you learn all this?' And he says with a swashbuckler's sly wink, 'I have my sources. And I've always been a determined character – determined to be more than just a dumb footballer.'

The rubbish sack is full. We've chatted our way around the whole site, cleaning up as we go. Owen has joined up with us. The conversation swung to Egypt in general and then, via Moses, we got onto plagues. It turns out Owen is some sort of plague specialist. He knows about locusts, rats, mice and lice, infestations of every kind. It appeals to him, the mass reproduction and suffocation of species. We're having afternoon tea and he entertains us all with gruesome details of the great disease plagues of history, bubonic and pneumonic, time frames of suffering, swellings and sores. Janet and Iris twist their faces as they butter pikelets and pour thermos water into cups balanced on the bonnet of the Landcruiser, but I'm the one who's shocked when I realise they aren't. They groan and grimace in play.

'We've heard it all before, Owen,' they say. 'You and your plagues.'

It makes me think they're not too bad.

He kids up to them.

'But have I told you about the buboes?' he says.

'Yes,' they chorus back.

'What's that?' I ask.

Gaynor and Alf roll their eyes and accuse me with mock despair, 'Were you the one who let him get started in the first place?'

'I wasn't to know,' I laugh.

'It's my fault,' says Bim, 'I'm the guilty party.' And he covers my hand briefly with his as if to remove the taint of blame.

'I'm always the guilty party,' he says, and grins.

Aren't people interesting creatures?

CHAPTER SIX
HERE COMES THE BRIDE

In the Coolie library it takes me an hour and a half to find out that Tolemy is spelt with a P. Ptolemy.

I change our books at the Coolie library every few weeks, Davey's spy thrillers and my nonfiction. It's one of the few after-work errands that I really look forward to. Strangely, there's also a sniff of disappointment just when I've reached the top of the pebblecrete stairs and I'm pushing open the glass doors. There should be ideas on the walls here, in lots of different colours, some scribbled and some written in neat hand but all crashing into each other. There should be ideas like poltergeists screaming at each other so you don't know which one to look at next and then yet another snatches at your hat and suddenly your head's as bare as a baby's.

But it's not like that. It's a big letdown. It's just grey paint and thin air. You could do your banking in here and you wouldn't be ashamed about paying so little off your mortgage.

Corridors and rows and rows of regulated books remind me of the names of dead soldiers which are stamped with such precision on the cold walls of the Canberra War

77

Memorial. You have to take the trouble to pick out a single name from that terrible ledger to smell sore feet in cracked boots, to see a sweat bead of malaria drip from a stubbled chin. And that's when I'm not disappointed anymore, when, at random, I take one book from a long shelf and I discover a life inside, find something I didn't know, or haven't ever felt. Then the anonymity of all those musty rows becomes a bonus, preserving powerful things for me to uncover.

In actual fact, what I mostly end up with, after all this grazing, are publications to do with other countries, places and peoples of the world – what we used to call Geography when I was at school. Though I don't read them cover to cover. I'm not so methodical. I skim, picking out snippets the way birds bob for seeds in fresh sown fields. Never mind if I sometimes miss important bits.

When I'm ready to get my library books stamped I usually shuffle around the counter for a bit, hoping to get served by the girl with all the things attached to her face. She fascinates me and scares me at the same time. She has two rings in her nose and four like rungs on a ladder stepping up the rim of her left ear. Looks like maybe one of the other ladies got to her with the stapler. As well, she often has a little tear-drop of plastic opal stuck to the middle of her forehead. She is thin with black crescents under her round eyes and always wears dark clothes, ominous purples. Once she had a little square of black net pinned to the top of her hair as if, when she finished her shift, she'd skip out to be married as a vampire bride.

She talks aloud and loudly to herself in the same bossy and cheerful sort of way that nurses often do, not looking at you, not expecting you to answer. She bosses the air while the other women behind the counter, dressed in pastel blouses and skirts, try to boss each other without each other knowing it.

The one thing they all have in common is the concerted effort they put into ignoring the mumbling public. They are an exclusive club inside the laminex coastline of their island counter. They've put up signs everywhere you look telling how to use this catalogue or that computer hoping no one will have to ask them personally for anything. It's not that they're lazy, they just have something else important to do. A man can't work a computer so there's an exasperated sigh and a finger raised to underline a sign as the senior librarian says, 'Continue search – yellow key. Restart – blue.' She doesn't have the time to waste on prepositions.

That's why I never asked them to help today with Ptolemy. I've been wanting to find out more about him ever since I heard of him a week ago.

I tried everything. I looked high and low for him; the catalogue (subject and author), encyclopaedias (Britannica and World Book), I even tried an enormous dictionary but there was nothing under T. Where was he, if he's so well known and popular? Just about defeated, I had a spark of Ptolemaic inspiration and looked up Alexandria. That's where I found him and his P. That's where I discovered not one but many Ptolemies, a whole family of them who ruled over ancient Egypt for hundreds of years. The dynasty ended with Cleopatra. Now there's someone I do know. And I found out something neat about that first lighthouse too. For fifteen centuries it stood in lovely Alexandria – fifteen centuries – until an earthquake brought it down.

It was Ptolemy Number Two who built the lighthouse, he was the smart one admired by Bim, he was the one who turned that old Egyptian city into the scientific and technological capital of the world.

I don't know if he was related, but there was yet another famous Ptolemy who came along a bit later on in the early ADs. Claudius Ptolemy. He was a mathematician, an astronomer and a geographer, so he was no slouch in the brains department either. He had this theory about space that everyone believed until the Renaissance. He reckoned the earth was the fixed centre of the universe and the heavenly bodies moved round it. It's a comforting view. But I've got my own theories about the cosmos.

I think there's a lot of trash written and said about the peacefulness of the night sky; the slow blink of a bevy of distant stars, the endless aching beauty of the ancient light that twinkles above. Try doing this. Lie down one night in the backyard (watch out in case the buffalo grass is damp or prickles through your clothes) and use the picket fence to provide the perimeter for your tunnel vision up to space. You'll need some sound. Maybe some kid next door is singing in the bath, a nursery rhyme. Follow the sound waves with your mind, travel with them up past the rooftops, round the globe, past the north pole and away up into the stars. By the time that singing kid is long past a great-grandmother, a long, long time past dead, her nursery rhyme will be out in space wandering round bumping into planets.

Except, you know – and this is my cobbled-together theory – it's not all nice and twinkly up there. That Old Mother Goose stuff will ricochet off Mars, and soar past

Saturn. It'll take a nick off Jupiter and punch out Neptune. Join in the chaos. Lying on your back in the backyard looking up. It's war up there, war and death.

There are nuclear explosions and implosions, gases leap from sun to sun, noxious clouds clamp moons, asteroids hurtle in search of a patch to bust up on, planets wobble out of flat tyre orbits, pick up speed and knock out stupid others, mortars of shooting stars and comets gouge fingernail trails, black holes perform their sleight of hand and take whole worlds prisoner. It's war. The lights we see are ghosts of the long dead. Wonder what's happening right now. What has come into being, what has ceased to exist. There are more numbers up there than you can poke a stick at but none of them make sense.

Maybe your Davey will come to the back door and stand in the yellow rectangle of light and call out, 'What are you doing out there, Lal?'

'Just looking at the night.'

The flyscreen might rattle open on its runners like mine does.

'Do you have to do it lying on your back?'

You shrug.

Maybe your Davey will come out and lie down beside you and look up.

We take in all those stars. You, me, and our Daveys. We take in all those stars. That may or may not be there.

'What's that kid singing?' they'll say.

I put some of the books back that I've found and keep a couple, one on the River Nile, and one about Aztec gold.

And then what always happens to me in the library happens. I've had enough. I'm ready to go. Suddenly it weighs me down, there are too many choices hovering in the stuffy layers of airconditioning. I need a breeze on my face and so much the better if it stings with the seaweed tang of low tide.

This is when I maybe understand why the library women are reluctant to leave their island, why the Vampire Bride glues the opal talisman to her head. There are too many big ideas in here. Too many choices. The cosmos, Ptolemy, Davey, Bim.

Click, click of the stamp inside the cover of each book, DUE BACK, and the Bride calls out to no one in particular, 'Next'.

CHAPTER SEVEN
SHOPPING WITH ONE BREATH

I'm at the corner shop and I'm standing on the footpath in between chewing gum spots and flattened cigarette butts taking a few relaxed breaths and waiting until the doorway's free. I'm just about to make my move when Iris and Bertie Marchant bustle out and Iris is smacking Bertie's wrist and hissing like a goose and it's clear she's not pleased. So I have to wait a little longer until she's smacked him well clear of the door. Then I take my big breath. I do it with my bottom jaw scooping up the air and then I clamp the gristle in my nose shut and I bolt into the shop.

I have to get my shopping done in this one breath. Milk and a block of cheese. Same refrigerator cabinet, then go straight to the counter with the right money ready in hand. Have a lip smile organised so you don't have to say hello. Not much time left. Counting in my head, fourteen, thirteen, twelve, to stretch the breath and make it last all the way down to one and out the door. Bertie Marchant! Nine, eight. He's back. He apologises as he slips in front of me. Six, five. He's leaning over the counter, stretching out his hand for a newspaper. 'Dollar forty, Marchant,' says Sullen Guts turning round from his hamburger cooking. Three, two, one, and one is hissing through my barely parted lips. I am defeated. I've been defeated before. The important thing now is to take very shallow breaths, sucking them in over my bottom row of teeth. Keep the nose shut. Bertie's leaning to one side, jangling deeper in his change pocket for another twenty cents. Be patient. Think of nothing. Sullen Guts has got his hands on his hips and a rivulet of sweat runs round his thick neck. While Bertie fossicks I push my money onto the counter and hold the milk and cheese up high like an Olympic torch to show Sullen Guts I'm not cheating. I'm out the door.

It takes a minute to recover and leaning against the telegraph pole helps. Looking out, the park in front of the town jetty is chipped with puddles the colour of old tea and the inlet beyond is a knocked-up browny-grey, the whole scene cuffed by a nasty June wind. Yeah the air's fresh, but it's all a little desolate. Sullen Guts has got his battered plastic table and chair set – his version of al fresco dining – tilted higgledy-piggledy and chained up to the rubbish bin on the footpath like some sort of slave family. They'll stay that way until spring. Above, the old Streets ice-cream sign swings from the awning, creaks with the breeze. We haven't had Streets ice-creams in Pocket Head for years. Sullen Guts never paid up on time so they stopped delivering. He's got some other brands in there but never all the ones on the pictures and the freezer's so frosted up that fishing for one is like sticking your hand down a yeti's throat.

I'm still looking up at the Streets sign when a voice says softly, 'What was that thing you were doing in there, with your mouth?'

'What?'

It's Bim Audette.

'I was watching you through the window.'

He's watching me now. He's looking at my lips. I can see them too as they open and close talking back to him. I can see him seeing how the lip skin sticks a little at the corners where they're dry.

'Breathing,' I say. 'I was breathing but I was trying not to.'

'Oh,' he says.

'I hate the smell of that shop – he never changes the cooking oil – and if you leave your mouth open the smell gets in and it's horrible if you have to swallow it.'

His lips are slightly windburnt. They say, 'You should use a scuba tank to do your shopping. Or at least have an Oxy Viva standing by.'

Bim Audette has green eyes flecked with brown. Like jetty water.

'If I ever see you turning blue on the footpath out here I'll know you've over-shopped.'

He's gone. My lips are dry and his are windburnt. He's gone into the shop. He's in no hurry. There's a rude beep from a car horn and Iris Marchant pulls up in their nifty little white Daihatsu. Bertie comes out of the shop, almost dropping his paper. He's half in and half out of the car when Iris rolls it forward a little so he's got to skip to get in. You shouldn't do that to a sixty-year-old man. They drive off.

The milk and cheese I've bought is cold in my hands. I wish I'd coped long enough with the shop-stink to snatch up a bag. I juggle the shopping from hand to hand, I'm a little stupefied after my encounter with Bim and have to will myself to get moving. Any minute he might spy me and wonder why I'm still standing on the wind-chilled street, never mind that I now appear to be practising a strange circus act involving dairy products.

I turn my back on the foreshore and the wind sends me hunched towards home, parting my hair in rough style and wrapping it in quick fingers round my face. Flicking fingers, warm touch – for an instant I am veiled, exotic, anonymous – and then I'm not. I'm me in a lemon uniform and a too-thin cotton knit trudging home after a day at work, with only more drudgery ahead; get the washing in, put the bins out, make a fish mornay dinner, wash up, watch the TV, go to bed. How did this happen? The smallness, the dullness of my life? Another gust bustles at me and I bow my head.

I fell in love with Davey because he had a motorbike. And sometimes he made me laugh at a time when, for a long while after Mum left, I thought I may have forgotten how. We'd take long rides on empty roads, the orange bark of the angophora gums flashing past like ignored traffic lights. We'd end up on some remote beach and settle on a picnic rug. And then it would be no, no, yes, yes. Not wanting to stop, too steamed up to stop, but knowing I was doing a foolish thing. Already knowing one day he'd sell his bike and some time after that I would have heard all his jokes twice. Knowing he wasn't the sort of man who could make up new ones.

No, no, but too steamed up to stop.

My body would not listen. It took control of my ears and shut down their function so I could not hear the future nagging, much less the squalling of seagulls or the hiss of water on sand. It shut the lids of my eyes against the sun so there was no sense of place, no sense from the senses except salt licked from skin.

No, no, but too steamed up to stop.

'It's alright,' Davey would say, cradling me in his honey-bear arms as protection against a cooling breeze. He seemed to sense my vulnerability. 'You need me, and I'm here.'

And Mum – how did she fall in love with Dad? I used to quiz her.

'I met your father in a train station,' she used to say. 'We had a cup of tea and then we got married.'

That was her – always making quick decisions. I used to laugh and say, 'You can't tell it like that – not a cup of tea and a wedding in the same mouthful! Tell the rest.'

'Well,' she'd say, pushing out a lot of air with the word as if you had to get out the stale stuff so you could take yourself back and remember freshly. 'I met your father at Central Station. It was winter, five o'clock and already dark. It was after work. I was letting myself get pushed along by the peak-hour mob, pushed against woollen coats and wet umbrellas. You couldn't see much ahead of you because it was a sea of hats, everyone wore hats to town in those days, and you had to watch your step because under your feet the grey concrete had turned muddy with the wet footprints of everyone going home. I got to the ramp leading up to my platform and looked up. There was your father. He was thanking a railwayman, juggling some parcels and a small suitcase to shake his hand, and as he turned to come down the ramp one of the parcels slipped. I can see that big brown paper bag tearing in slow motion as he snatched after it. And tumbling out of it came a dozen oranges bouncing down the steep slope. His lips made a big slow-motion O of surprise. Then he scurried after them like a clown collecting up a trick that had gone wrong. He was excuse-me-ing and laughing with embarrassment as he dived between people's legs for the oranges. I collected up what I could for him, they were beautiful bright things and such a size so as one would fill your whole palm. We had them tucked in our arms and under our chins when we met and your father said thank you, smiling. Though I could hardly hear him because of the underground din of the tunnels filled with people and the rumble of trains. He made a little "follow me" nod with his head. It was only a little nod because otherwise the orange under his chin would have got loose. We jostled our way out of the throng to the country trains area, and dumped our loads onto a little table in the tea rooms there. The waitress was a cranky sort of girl, sour and suspicious, I suppose because she spent her whole day stuck in a place designed for departures, yet she never went anywhere. She came rushing over with a "what do you think you're up to" look on her face and said threateningly, "Tea?" I don't think your father was game to say no. I minded the table full of oranges while your father went across to the man at the fruit barrow to ask for some bags. When he came back the cranky girl was trying to set down the teacups in between the oranges. So that's how we came to be drinking tea together.'

This is the part where she usually stopped. As if this was the end. This is the part where she needed a push.

'But what was he doing there? With the oranges?'

'Oh, he'd come down from Pocket Head to visit his aunt. Stay with her actually, while he had a temporary job at the Mortlake Works. He was in the wrong place entirely. The wrong platform to get to Lewisham where she lived. But it didn't seem to matter to him. He was open-faced and full of … optimism, I suppose it was.'

'But from the cup of tea to the wedding, what happened in between?'

'Oh, we went out to dances and picnics, that sort of thing. Your father always had plans. He'd hang round the door of the office with his hat in his hand, waiting for five o'clock to tick over. We girls would empty out of the typing pool and he'd grab my hand and say, "Let's skedaddle." Maybe he'd say, "Let's go to Bondi for fresh air and fish and chips." The beach always reminded him of home and he'd talk about Pocket Head. He made it sound idyllic.'

It was never much good from here on in. I'd say, 'And what happened then?' And she'd always say, 'Then he asked me to marry him and then I said yes.'

'And then you lived happily ever after,' I'd finish for her.

'Yes,' she'd say.

But each time she told the story a different colour attached itself to that last single word.

When I think about it, it seems arbitrary, the way our lives are formed, at least for me. I don't seem to have made many decisions.

I'm home. I check the letterbox for mail, then go round the back and dump everything down on the outdoor table so I can fumble in my handbag for the key. Davey and I have decided we'd better start locking up, though half the time I forget. My cold fingers aren't working well. Finally, I get the door open but I don't step, can't step, straight in. It's still and quiet and dark inside. My empty house.

CHAPTER EIGHT
A GOOD TURN

I made a fool of myself this afternoon. I went to the
Audette's house. They don't have just a front porch, they
have an entrance area like the front door of a big hotel.
Tiles and huge pots from another country, Ali Baba pots,
but with reeds, not thieves, stretching their arms out from
them. The door was open, a great chunk of wood it was, as
if hewn from the one monstrous tree trunk. My hand
looked silly clenched in a little fist to knock on that vast
polished surface. It didn't seem likely my knock would
travel anywhere much, just get sucked in and stuck in the
grain of the door. I thought if I have to call out I might just
go home instead. They needed a doorbell.

I knocked.

'Who is it?' she called out almost immediately. 'Come
down to the living room, I'm in the living room.'

I set off down the wide tiled entrance hall and it seemed
more like a launch pad into space because dead ahead was
a railing, air and then a huge spread of blue (mostly sky but
some sea) through windows as huge and pointed at the top
as ones in a cathedral. There were only thin strips of metal
between the soaring panes and I don't know how they held

the glass steady. I looked over the stainless steel railing of the launch pad, down to an acre of cream carpet below, and there, lying on a cream lounge as isolated as a lifeboat cast adrift, was Barbara Audette.

'I'm Lal,' I said, venturing it out with an echo clinging to it.

'Are you,' she replied.

Her face was angled up to me.

'I live down the bayside, I've seen you round.'

Thick dark hair framed her face. An expensive cut. French-looking.

'I'm in the Historical Society,' I babbled on. 'At the last meeting Bim mentioned you were sick and I'm sorry. I mean sometimes I help, with ironing. I'm a good ironer and I just take it away and iron it if that helps.'

'Ironing,' said those lips up to me, moving but unmoved.

My offer seemed increasingly strange to me, though it never had before. But she didn't seem fazed, only reached over for a packet of cigarettes on the glass-topped coffee table and lit one.

'Is it your job?' she said, blowing out the first smoke.

'No, no, I've got a job,' I said, hanging onto the railing, and painfully aware my credentials wouldn't be improved by mentioning the lunch shop in Coolie. 'Ironing is just something to help, if people can't manage for themselves for a time. When they're sick.'

'But I'm not sick.'

'Oh. Right.'

A pause.

'Just had my veins done,' she called out in a louder, theatre sort of voice.

I could see crisp white bandages on her legs which were poking out from the bottom of her terry-towelling robe.

'Perhaps,' she said, 'you had better come down, Lal.'

'Do you do it to look?' she said as I got to the bottom of the stairs and was approaching the lifeboat lounge.

'Pardon?' I asked.

'Do you do it to look into other people's lives?'

'Oh no. I don't think so.'

Flicking some ash into the ashtray she said, 'Do you know, you don't sound so sure.'

'Well, I never have before. It's just ironing. Perhaps you shouldn't have said it,' I replied.

'Why?' she said.

'Because now you've said it, I might start thinking it. Oh, not about you, I mean, just in general.' I felt a red blush of embarrassment creep up my neck and beads of nervous sweat prickled on my brow.

She laughed.

She wasn't helping. Not one little bit.

I was stranded in the middle of all that carpet, didn't know whether to sit or where to sit even. They could do with more furniture. Didn't want to sit anyway. It would seem like grovelling. I went over to the window right up to the edge and then immediately jumped back a foot because I felt I might just tip out and down into the scrub forty feet below.

There was a lot of life out that window.

The yellow gash of beach was arranged in front and below of you. Close inshore the water was white and green, changing to blue as you tilted up to the denim smear of the horizon at eye level. From this vantage point you had to remind yourself that the water was really on a horizontal plane and not a vertical one. It seemed miraculous that it stayed in place and didn't come pouring down from the horizon in a great wave, flooding the beach, the bush, and smashing this flimsy old plate glass into smithereens. I saw a vision of Barbara surfing the crest on her cream couch screaming helplessly and shards of glass from the windows poking up from the sea around her like the fins of sharks.

That window was like a giant cinema screen only it would operate twenty-four hours a day. If I was ever to offer that smart Barbara a piece of advice it would be, get some curtains. With some curtains it would be easier to keep your right size.

'It's too much, isn't it?' she said suddenly into the silence and I spun round.

She had the cigarette poised in the air, the ash was an inch long and ready to drop but just in time she paid attention and stubbed it out.

'Do your legs hurt?' I asked, speaking in my real voice for the first time.

'Not much. Sometimes. I don't think there is much ironing,' she said. 'I've been in robes, and Bim's things … well, I said he could go wrinkly. But it would be kind of you to do what there is.'

I can't believe I went there and made a fool of myself like that. I've cut my finger twice thinking about it. I must have been mad. What did I think I was doing? She's a rich woman, she could pay someone to do her housework.

And now Davey's late. He knows I can't bear anyone to be late. Late is bad. He knows he has to ring the minute he's aware he'll be delayed.

As a distraction I try to concentrate on the chequerboard of a crossword puzzle. I've been making a salad and must scrape away the vegie scraps to another part of the newspaper to read the clue to eleven across. 'A little song.' With the big tip of the knife I press D.I.T.T.Y into the newspaper. Gloop, gloop goes the red mince of the bolognaise. Heat from the stove at my elbow. I wonder what Barbara Audette is having for dinner. Four down. 'South African mollusc.' The point of the knife is silent. Twenty-two across. 'Roman babe raised by wolves.' The stainless steel hangs and quivers but will not move ouija-style until I catch the clue to seven down, 'After midday' – P.M it stabs. And finally Davey's ute rattles down the drive.

I remove the board and fold the puzzle and the scraps in on themselves and post the neat parcel of newspaper through the flap of the kitchen bin. I'm waiting for the sound of boots on the porch, for the loud sniff at kitchen smells as he passes the window, for the voice to boom to the neighbour's and back with the nightly mantra, 'Yum, my favourite.' But there is nothing. Just the bubble of bolognaise. Through the black back window the tail-lights of the ute still glow red out in the garage like the smouldering tips of cigarettes. Plates in the oven and the salad and the shaker of stink-cheese on the table and still no boots.

I get a cardigan and pull it tight over my breasts against the wintery night and go out to the garage. Davey is slumped in the driver's seat, hands on the wheel. He's ashen faced and wide eyed.

'I've killed Question Mark Man,' he says in a flat voice. 'The coppers will be round later to make an arrest.'

I get him inside, I sit him down at the kitchen table, I

ask him what happened, I say to him, 'Just tell me what happened.'

The stone of disbelief in his face begins to crack. 'I mowed him down. Didn't see him, he was walking by. I was backing out of Col's driveway. Went too fast, joking with Col about the Grand Prix. Oh God. Question Mark Man – he's a goner, Lal.' Davey hides his face in his hands.

'I've taken a life by showing off and I'll be jailed.'

A Bush Fire Brigade car turned up and they loaded in Question Mark and sped off, siren screaming. Davey was left in a daze.

'So Question Mark Man must be alright if they put the siren on,' I say gently to Davey.

'Yes, no,' says Davey. 'He was unconscious, with blood coming out of his head. I knocked him and he fell pretty hard, he could be in a bad way.'

I want Davey to ring the hospital but he won't, he reckons they'll only speak to next of kin.

'The coppers will tell us, they'll be here with handcuffs soon for sure.' Davey slumps into a puddle of remorse. 'The poor man ... I've hurt a defenceless thing.'

Question Mark Man. Lying alone and battered in Coolie Hospital, the life oozing out of him while the staff watch helplessly, unable to put it back. It's awful. Davey, what have you done? I'd miss Question Mark, I realise. On my walks. He is innocence abroad and it's a terrible thing to contemplate the loss of innocence.

I don't know what to do, so, like an automaton, I put the dinner on the table.

'Could be my last decent meal,' says Davey, staring at the plate.

He's starting to get to me. For a minute I allow myself to contemplate it – my husband, the killer. What would life be like punctuated by prison visits?

'It was an accident, Davey,' I say to remind us both.

Davey rocks back in his chair and picks up a box of matches from the bench near the stove. Strikes one. It sparks and flares. He turns the match in his fingers, adjusting it so the flame eats the wood down to the dirt in his nails. He doesn't ouch when the last of it nips at his skin. Just puffs his lips to push out the last weak blue of fire. He examines the black curl of what is left, so thin at one point, how could it stay whole?

He says quietly, 'Maybe I understand you a bit better now, Lal, why you worry about things. Now I know myself how quickly life can change.'

He flips the dead match into the plate of spaghetti bolognaise and reaches for another from the box.

'Who would believe the back of a ute could do so much damage?'

He's going do the whole boxful, I know, and turn his dinner into some kind of culinary echidna.

'I'm ringing the hospital,' I say.

When I turn back from the admissions desk, Davey has a baby in his arms. It's crying, whaa, whaa. It is red and wrinkle-browed, its mouth pulled in an oblong slot and its arms are out of its rug in a stiff-elbowed protest. Little fingers curl to pretend at fists. Davey is chug-a-lugging and google-garing and jiggling it up and down.

'Come on, little fella it's alright, little man, come on now.'

'What are you doing,' I hiss. It's crossed my mind he might have stolen it as some sort of extravagant diversionary tactic to avoid the crisis at hand.

'Where's the mother?'

Whaa, whaa.

He wrenches his neck. 'In the toilet. I'm doing her a favour. Question Mark Man, is he alright?'

'Come to Aunty Lal, you poor little thing.'

'Is he still alive?'

Whaa, whaa.

'They've got him parked up the corridor waiting to go to X-ray.'

'Oh God, broken bones – what if I've broken every bone in his body?'

'Shush, little one, Mummy will be back in a minute. Shush now.'

Whaa, whaa.

'How many broken bones, Lal?'

'I don't know, Davey, they haven't done the X-ray yet. Go and ask him how many feel broken, he's just up the corridor.'

Whaa, whaa.

'Give me that baby,' he says, snatching it back from me. 'I can't,' he whinges. 'I can't talk to him, I ran him over. Besides, I'm minding the baby. What could I say to him?'

Whaa, whaa.

'Just go and talk to him. You can't leave him there all on his own. Here's the mother.'

Davey hands the baby over. By now it's beetroot-coloured.

'I'm sorry, I tried. Back to Mummy, little fella.'

'It's a girl,' says the mother, offended, and she yanks the

rug down to display more of the predominantly pink romper suit as proof. Then she pinches up her nose at Davey and shows him her back.

'How's that for thanks!' he says.

'Come on,' I say.

The corridor is busy. Blood and cuts wander past sprouting in red blooms on white gowns and bandages. An old woman parked in a wheelchair retches into a kidney dish and then comes up for air, dabbing her mouth with a tissue. Question Mark Man lies, a stretch of body as long as a mile of road, on a hospital trolley.

I hold Davey's hand tighter as we approach. Question Mark can't see us, he's staring at the scuff marks on the wall. When we get to the trolley I nudge Davey to speak but he's whiter than the lady in the wheelchair and his lips clamp shut. I touch Question Mark on the shoulder and he's startled but his face relaxes when he recognises mine. He's got a whopping great bandage on his head.

'How are you,' I say.

'I am okay?'

'Are you?'

'I think that I may not paint for a week but that isn't so bad?'

'Isn't it?'

I kick Davey in the ankle to make him talk.

'They say I need some stitching and my elbow bone may be chipped, so it seems I shall miss out on the competition.'

'What competition is that, mate?' asks Davey in a croaky voice.

'I should defend the championship, no? Tomorrow night, state championship, mah jong?'

'Jesus, sorry, mate,' says Davey. 'Didn't know you were a champion.'

Davey looks impressed and mouths to me, 'Martial arts.'

The dog!

It's daybreak and I wake with a start, instantly alert the way a fireman must be when the fire bell goes off. I whack Davey on the chest.

'The dog!'

'Ow,' he grunts. 'Whatcha do that for? Go back to sleep.'

'You're hopeless. You're a selfish bastard.'

I'm out of the bed pulling on clothes.

'Last night you promised Question Mark Man you'd find his dog and look after it until he got out of hospital.'

Where's a jumper, it's chilly.

'But oh no, you were so full of laughter and chat on the way home, so relieved you hadn't killed him, you forgot all about it.'

'So did you.'

'I didn't run him over.'

The bottom of the wardrobe is a shambles and I'm raking over shoes, trying to find a matching pair.

'Why can't you be responsible for once? You just don't want to get out of a warm bed. That poor dog will be lonely and confused – traumatised – without his master.'

'Lal, it's six o'clock in the morning. The dog'll still be asleep. I'll go later.'

'Yeah, sure.' And I fire off a shoe that doesn't match and it rotates through the air and clips him neatly on the ear.

*   *   *

Morning light ricochets off walls, spears of gloss turn and
spin towards me. Crisp blue and white, I blink it back. I
step into the front room of Question Mark Man's house.
It's beautiful. Patchworked with postcards of coasts and
skies and seas from all the places of the world. In the middle
of the room is a vinyl swivel chair and a television set, an
old one, it must be black-and-white. A two-seater couch
placed to face the windows.

But it's also shocking to stand in the middle of all that
nakedness. The emptiness of it, the rest of the world pasted
on the walls and only one small person watching.

There is a click click, no hurry, of toenails on the wooden
floor, and I turn to see Black Dog picking through the
doorway. He doesn't tread on any cracks between the floorboards, I swear. He stops three feet from me and smiles loll-
tongueingly round the room, proud of the survey. He
doesn't seem confused by his master's absence. To the con-
trary, he brings in a completeness: the welcome of a host.

I wander through the house, having Black Dog as a guide
makes it seem alright. Everything is neat and functional in
Question Mark Man's wooden house among the trees. He's
got one of those Japanese beds in his bedroom, the ones
that are like sleeping on garden furniture, and a cupboard
and that's all. Then there's a workroom; I always thought
he must work from home. It turns out he's an artist. There's
an easel and a big drafting desk and a bench along one wall
with all manner of drawing and painting equipment set out
along it. And then it dawns on me. He paints greeting cards.
Happy Birthday. On Your 25th Wedding Anniversary.
Thinking Of You. To A Special Grandpa. His designs are
lying about in different stages of completion. There're

flowers, and hedgehogs with soccer balls, men on golf courses, warmly clad against autumn cold, and sailboats on lakes, their sails smart with wind. He's very talented. Lucky Davey didn't do too much damage, it would be terrible to be responsible for ruining an artist's career. Like causing a different sort of death.

Black Dog and I step out into Pocket morning streets, early stirrings. There's Gary Musselbrook driving off to work, blue smoke coming out of his exhaust, he wants to get that fixed, and there're the blinds going up in Number 23. A white cat on a fence licks its paw. Black Dog takes no notice but pads alongside happily.

'Are you hungry, boy-o?' I say.

He nods as he walks. He's an old man in fur.

'How about spaghetti bolognaise for breakfast?' I ask.

We're passing in front of Rosie Lunt's place and right on cue she opens up the door and comes on out, fully dressed, a teapot in her hand. She gives us a curt nod, Rosie's not one to muck round, and Black Dog waves his tail back and I wave my hand. She swills the tea-leaves out into the garden, maybe she's getting ready for a quick second pot, there's steam coming up from the warm dregs splattered among the plants. She looks like she's been up for hours. Most old people are early risers. Not Dad though. There won't be any action round at his house for ages yet.

Dad gradually got into the habit of sleeping in after Mum left. He started staying up until all hours. I'd come in late after having been out with Davey and find him hunched over the radio listening to late-night talkback shows. I'm not sure if he was listening for clues or trying to dilute his hurt in the sad wash of all-night radio waves, but the intimate outpourings of strangers seemed to make him feel better. That was fine by me because in the beginning he was a mess. He just cried quietly in corners of the house. I'd go into a room and find him facing a wall, not touching it, his arms straight down by his sides. Tiny movements of his shoulders as he sobbed up and down, a sound so small it may as well have not been there at all. I'd walk out like I'd never been there or seen there the shaking of my father's shoulders.

I regret it. It was my big mistake and the passing years have made it bigger, but I needed him to comfort me, and I let the cleft of unshared hurt rest between us.

When I wanted to search for her he said with spit and venom, 'Keep waiting. She's coming back.'

He made me feel my doubt was reprehensible.

He never tried to give an explanation for her going, or even make one up. He just grieved as if she had been stolen by aliens and did not dare speak of it because no one would believe him.

Well, I don't think that happened. Not for one half of a second do I think aliens stole her. But just make that imaginative leap. Just *imagine* they did. Pretend it's not stupid that they came into the kitchen and made her write the note. How lonely would it be to know no one would ever save you because their imaginations were too small. She could be spinning round on a red planet somewhere way away on the edge of space – she could be an inhabitant of a space station zoo. Enclosed in a white cell with a perspex window. And strolling by are elegant ETs, smiling admiringly at her. Or perhaps they shudder and cringe from the sight of her; she might be locked in the equivalent of a reptile house where visitors go to enjoy being repulsed. At feeding time a keeper tosses in a roast dinner with contempt, as if it's excrement. Either way, Mum is forlorn, shrivelled in a corner, languishing for want of a window overlooking earth. She's longing for the blue sky and the green sea, for the smell of concrete paths dotted with the first big spots of rain. She's worried who will remind Dad to cut the lawn and have I pierced my ears. And who will ever know she's there, she can't send a postcard and it's not likely that NASA will come bumbling by, see her and bring her home.

Of course, it's possible too that she likes it. She may have been scared at first when they stole her out of the kitchen so unexpectedly. But when they installed her in an exotic court as a favoured guest it became fun. And now she shakes her head slowly when they kindly offer her a return ticket.

The funny thing is I don't remember what she looks like. I mean, I do. When I look at a photo my brain says yes she looked exactly like that. But when I'm away from photos I can only see the shape of her, the silhouette. I saw a man once at the Easter Show cut out silhouette portraits from black paper and mount them onto white. His short fat fingers were stubbed into barber's scissors like half-smoked cigarettes into an ashtray. He trimmed features like hair. It was fast and oh so precise and no customer walked away without a new-found snub nose. Everyone looked different, a bit like themselves, but a lot like the plaque on a rest room door. Mum's like that when I try to remember without a photo. There's the shadow of her, but not much more. It doesn't matter if I try to recall something general, like how she looked on a wet day when she was blue, or something specific, like her face that time we were walking by the bay and a fish jumped and caught us by surprise. I only have left the *feeling* of what she looked like on those occasions. I can see more of me looking than of her being.

The really strange thing is that in the later photos she's roundabout about the same age I am now. So if I meet someone in the street, my contemporary, who looks a bit like her, I'm liable to think, 'This may be Mum I'm talking to.' Except, of course, it couldn't be. But she'd still have the same concerns as me, most likely. The same shopping in her trolley and a similar amount on Bankcard. I bet our shopping is really very similar. It took me a long time to buy a different brand of mustard, even though it tasted better, because it seemed a betrayal. A betrayal of taste.

Every once in a while, maybe five times a year, I do see her. In a dream. I'm dreaming along about something quite ordinary and there she is. Exactly. Like in a video. She turns round and the back of her is as true as the front. You think, yes, my God, she did walk like that, and yes, she did tuck her long hair behind her ears ruefully when it wasn't tied back. And then she's sitting opposite me at the table, both hands together in a loose prayer but pointed towards me, not heaven. It's a generous motion, the V of her fingers parts the air either side of it and the little fingers tap the table gently but insistently.

At first I wake up happy, excited. Like all I have to do is look and of course there'll be more milk in the fridge. As the minutes go by I lie straighter in bed. Hope emptying out and replaced with guilt. I'm ashamed because there she'd been so real and I, now that I'm awake, can't remember something as fundamental as a familiar mannerism. That's when I kick myself and make a pledge to remember better. I won't allow the slow fade of time to take her away further because then it would be me abandoning her.

I take a tissue from the pocket of the yesterday's pants I'm wearing. It must be the sharp morning air that makes my eyes water and my nose run. Black Dog stops to sniff at a fence post. It seems polite to wait. Do you know they say dogs have got a memory for over two hundred thousand different smells? Black Dog snuffles then cocks his leg to obliterate whichever numbered one was there.

Anyway, I might not have had my mum for as long as I would have liked but I try not to keep on living in the hurt. Imagine if you never had a mother at all, or you got stuck with a horrible, cruel one, or even one like Barbara Audette. Urgh. It'd be like having a swordfish for a mother. Not the sort of woman I'd pictured for Bim Audette.

I've still got to face up to her ironing yet. Barbara's right to question my motives, I'm not a good Samaritan, I'm a goon.

The day at work drags by and I'm distracted, serving the wrong takeaways and giving the wrong sandwiches to the wrong tables. In front of the punters, the boss snaps, 'What's got into you!'

I'm thinking about Question Mark Man and I'm also wondering about Black Dog, how he feels, fenced in the unfamiliar square of our backyard. During a break I ring the hospital and they tell me they've sent Question Mark home. The X-rays revealed no broken bones and they only kept him in for observation because of his concussion, since he lives on his own. I reckon he'll want to see his canine friend as soon as possible.

In the afternoon Black Dog and I trot off again and wind down the overgrown path which at first reveals only glimpses of Question Mark Man's house. A side wall, a hint of roof, a back wall, seen through bushes. Windows are open, the back door's open, breathing in the trees and breathing out lilting music of strings and pipes and voices in an unfamiliar language.

Black Dog quickens his step, coming home, sniffs at notes. Pausing on the doormat on the flagstones it seems a bigger trespass to call out hello than to enter. It is hypnotic, that music, from some still country that doesn't know wind.

We patter across the floorboards, Black Dog and I, into the big room with the postcards where Question Mark Man lies curled up on the couch, looking out the windows at the green.

'You are here?' he says and he smiles and nods into the music.

Black Dog stands for a brief eye-blinking head pat from his master and then slumps in an untidy heap on the floor against the couch.

'How do you feel?' I say, keeping the words quiet and putting them into the plenty big enough gaps between the instruments.

Again he nods.

'This room is wonderful,' I say.

I drift over to the postcard-covered walls and comb over the pictures. So many. So many places.

'How come they're all from places on the coast?' I ask.

'Ten pen friends, I have, for many years? It was a

coincidence at first when they sent me these from their holidays but then I said in my replies, this is good, I live by the sea but have no view of it, only trees. Now they seek them out on purpose. It is nice to be an island in the ocean?'

'Yes, it's nice.'

'And I always have good weather in here!'

Vladivostok, the Sandwich Islands, Hudson Bay. Reykjavik and Vera Cruz. Port Elizabeth and Port Said. Gulfs and seas, channels, canals, isles and capes and archipelagos. Straits and passages.

Question Mark Man shuts his eyes to drink the music. A big upturned lippy smile of sweetness sculpts his face. He has the dome of Buddha and I see that he is older than I thought. A thousand-year-old egg.

'Do you hear this part,' he says with his eyes still shut, 'where the notes stretch?'

He says it reminds him of a woman he knew once, she was slim and willowy like that. 'I will grow a tomato for you,' he'd said to her. The roundest, reddest tomato would be for her. 'I will present it to you in the palm of my hand,' he'd said. 'And it will smell of leaf and earth.'

But it seems she did not think a vegetable was such a good present.

He smiles even more.

Question Mark Man is a puzzle with no pieces missing, a puzzle that doesn't need solving. He's like a lizard or a rock or a child without guile – he's a kaleidoscope – simple and complicated at the same time.

Black Dog starts to snore.

CHAPTER NINE

TAKEAWAY

I'm at the Bowling Club. Mai's telling me this story how she goes to Dr Ranold's to get her youngest's leg stitched on Tuesday after she fell off her bike. She's saying, 'Lal, I'm in such a bloody hurry I don't shut Ranold's front gate. I'm crying out, "Doctor, quick, you fix my girl's leg." His little dog has run out the front door quick smart and is doing circles and yapping its head off and pissing all at same time. I've got Annie in my arms and blood's pouring out and I say, "See my Annie!" And that bastard Ranold rushes out after the dog, he's calling, "Whiskey! Whiskey! Come back inside," and I put Annie down and run after him. Ranold is heading out the gate and I scream at the top of my lungs, "Forget the bloody dog. You look after my daughter or I will catch the bloody dog and turn him into Chihuahua Chow Mein!" After Annie has her three stitches and I relax, I tell Ranold, "You want to look after that little dog. I seen one at the beach one day get eaten by a pelican. One mouthful."'

'Ha hee,' and Mai and I are laughing our guts out imagining Ranold chasing a pelican down the beach with Whiskey's tail hanging out of its beak when Davey yells out, 'Put a sock in it, Lal. We're trying to concentrate.'

He's playing darts and it's comp night. The Commercial Hotel team from Coolie are running rings round them.

'Big man, little dart,' giggles Mai and I'm hooting with laughter all over again.

'Gee, mate,' says a grubby little coot from the Commercial team, 'your missus really does what she's told.'

'Shut up, Roach,' Davey says.

'Make me,' says Roach, 'I'm really frightened. You can't even shut ya missus up.'

'Oh for God's sake,' I say. 'I'm going home.'

I can't stand being that close to so much stupidity. Davey comes over to the bar on the pretext of buying a round but he's slipped the car keys onto the counter and out of the corner of his mouth he says, 'Take the car.'

'I don't want the car,' I say, 'I'm going to walk.'

'Take the car.'

'No.'

'I don't want you wandering round at night on your own.'

'I don't care what you want me to do,' I say.

'Besides, I've probably had too much to drink now, so I can't drive. You take the car.'

In the middle of all this Mai drifts off to serve a takeaway customer. It's Bim Audette.

'So, really, you only want me to take the car because it's more convenient for you,' I say. 'The wife'll take care of it.'

'Get stuffed,' he says, and he turns heel and walks away leaving the car keys in a spillage of beer on the bar.

I'm so angry I have just got to concentrate. I watch my Diana Ferrari shoes take one fast step after another over changing terrain, first the wooden slats of the club verandah, then the potholes in the car park, then the concrete of the

footpath, and I don't even care if I tread on the cracks.
I'm walking so fast my tailwind would even put Question
Mark Man into a spin. I'm humiliated. I've stormed off
leaving them to snigger a victory snigger behind their
nicotine-stained hands and Davey's going to be the brunt
of all their dumb jokes all night. He'll be embarrassed by
me for nothing and how dare he. I don't want to look up
from the ground because I know the bay will melt my
anger. The lights will be tearing across the still water and just
now I don't want to see something that beautiful. So instead
I'm watching the smoke rising from my Diana Ferraris,
thinking pretty soon the footpath's going to catch flames
and become a blazing trail right up to the front door of
my house.

Then, just when I'm about to cross another driveway, a
black car swings in front of me and stops, blocking my
path. The driver's window sinks open. Then Bim Audette's
teeth say, 'Are you alright? Looks like you're in a hurry.
Can I drive you somewhere?'

'No you cannot!' I snap back.

He sort of shrinks his neck back inside the car like a
tortoise but he isn't frightened. Looks like he might even
smile but I swear I'll wipe it off his face if he dares.
He doesn't say anything, just waits like I owe him an
explanation.

'You got a takeaway,' I say finally.

'Yes, I did.'

'Honey King Prawns?'

Davey always orders Honey King Prawns.

'Nope. I'm allergic to seafood,' he says. 'Is this a guessing
game?'

'No.' Which is just as well because I'm not much good at games.

In the absence of knowing what else to say I look up and out at the bay and, yes, it sure is beautiful. There's a trawler poking its nose out round False Point and making way towards the entrance to the open sea. They've got some music playing which floats over here but it's kind of bumping into itself so I can't make out the tune.

'If you're not late for an appointment or anything, I'd like to show you something. Can you be trusted?'

He's talking to me, I realise. For no reason I suddenly think, oh God, I hope he didn't see my arse wobble. When I was walking down the road so quickly my bottom would have been rolling from side to side and up and down like a bathtub caught in a cross swell. I shuffle round the car to the passenger side and get in. If I'm sitting on it, he can't notice it, my large arse. I sink into the seat. It's plush. It might be leather.

'What sort of car is this?' I ask.

'A BMW.'

Wait until I tell Davey.

We glide off, me with Bim Audette in Bim Audette's black car. I can't think of anything else to say. We are silent until Bim points into the dark at the first house in Ridge Road and asks, 'Do you know who lives in there?'

'Yeah, that's the Nobles'.'

'Best block in town,' he says. 'You could bulldoze that and get views both ways – bay and beach.'

He swings the car round the next bend and I have to hang onto the armrest to steady myself.

'That's a solid brick house,' I say. 'You can't bulldoze that.

It's only eight years old.'

'The Nobles built that ugly thing?'

'Yeah, after they got their old one burnt down for a case of cans and two hundred dollars.'

'What?' he laughs, not believing me.

'It's true. Everyone knows it. A bloke from Newcastle did the job.'

We pull into Bim's driveway and he reaches for the magic button to open up the garage door.

'You ought to get his phone number!' he says, and he thinks it's funny.

I look at him sharply but he's peering over the bonnet of the car, inching the vehicle right up to the back wall of the garage, the headlight beams reduced to disks.

'What are we doing here, anyway,' I say, not inclined to shift.

'Come on.'

He grabs the takeaway bag from the back seat and swings it into the front, stirring its aromas.

'Chicken and Cashews,' I say.

He says, 'You've got a great nose.'

Bim Audette is an interesting mixture of a man. I can't put my finger on what it is that makes him different. There's a certain kind of power at rest under his clothes. We're in the house and I have to skip a bit, almost trot, to keep up with him as he strides along. He doesn't turn on any lights but he moves with sureness, as if he can see plain as day in the dark. In the lounge room, with those big windows, everything is bathed in grey from the moon, but this return to vision is short lived as we head down some stairs to a third level. There are vague shapes on the stairwell walls, sporting memorabilia, I think, framed jerseys and medals, but I don't pause for fear I'll trip in the narrowing dark. I watch Bim's heels on the treads and put my feet exactly where his have been. We might be going down the shaft of a coalmine. Perhaps that's where Bim gets all his wealth; though the Auto Acre is a reasonably sized business you wouldn't think it would pay for all of this.

'Where's your wife?' I ask, thinking maybe Barbara's down there in a miner's hat, chipping away at the black stuff with a canary singing in a cage until the gas gets its tongue.

'She's bored with her convalescence. She's staying in the city. With her sister. They'll be drinking martinis and bad-mouthing me. They're a pair of harridans.'

Being a harridan sounds bad, he huffs it out. Maybe I underestimated Barbara as a swordfish.

Bim turns around a corner, opens some double doors, flicks a light switch. Bing. We are somewhere strange. A gallery, a wide corridor, a windowless place with cones of white light glowing on and in glass cabinets which are arranged along one wall. And at the far end is a massive wooden statue of a woman. It's a figurehead from an old sailing ship. She dominates it all. Bim takes my elbow to guide me to the first cabinet, and to restrain me from an instinctive urge to go to the wooden woman first. She is magnetic.

This place seems to be a private museum. The first cabinet has whaling tools in it, harpoons, one twisted like a corkscrew from some horrible battle for life, and three pieces of scrimshaw, black tattoos on fishes' teeth. While I read the neatly typed labels, Bim opens the lid of his takeaway and tucks in with plastic chopsticks. He works them like an expert, raking the food into a neat pile and balancing it on the ends.

The next cabinet has a set of manacles used on convicts who misbehaved at work during construction of the Pocket Head lighthouse. There are various old bottles, some coins, a pair of soldier's boots. A musket gun. A hat made from wallaby skin with the animal's ears attached. It belonged to the first and only Merrengong harbourmaster and he sewed it himself, invisible stitches buried in fur. I look at Bim, and while he chews up a big mouthful of chicken and cashews, he cocks his head at me to ask the question, 'Well, what do you think?'

What I think is it's no wonder the Coolie museum is half empty – he's got everything! He's got a cabinet of bits and pieces from the pioneering days, even things belonging to the Acton family, children's samplers, a bible, a christening cup, a pair of spectacles, a necklace with green jewels. He's got an original painting of Coolie as seen from Combyne Hill in 1890 (but it's not that good, there's a tree with branches thicker than the trunk). He's got the ship's bell from the wreck of the *Angel*.

'But that's in the foyer of the Council Chambers,' I say to him. 'How can you have one too?'

'Theirs is a replica. Naturally, the *Angel* is of special interest to me. I helped Mayor Acton out with a little financial problem he had and he agreed to sell the original. But, Lal,' he says, 'I tell you this in strictest confidence.'

'If you ask me,' I say, 'it smacks of larceny.'

He splutters on a chopstick load of fried rice. 'Not at all, not at all. It's business.'

'And this,' I say, finally free to head towards the wooden

lady, 'how did you come by this? Did you just pop her under your arm and nick her from the National Maritime Museum when nobody was looking?'

She's beautiful.

We stand and gaze at her.

She has long golden hair, curled with wind, a high rounded brow and a fine pointed nose, brown lips, pale skin. Her paint is chipped in many places, the colour gone dull, and this might make her fragile, except her expression is striking. Resolute. Her eyes could X-ray waves, pierce clouds, dissolve lines of horizons, send sea monsters scurrying for poky caves. They are eyes which would never once look back for land. In her left hand shines a star to light the way.

'Her name is Liberty,' says Bim.

He reaches up and puts his palm upon her breast, its full shape swelling beneath her flimsy dress, and then he moves, slithers his hand down to her hips where her legs, her gown, melt – transform into a functional lump, part of the rough timber of the bow.

I can't take my eyes off her. I would like to see the things she sees. I would like Bim Audette to touch me the way he touches her.

Can I be trusted, he'd asked me earlier. It is an unexpected thing to learn in Bim's museum that I cannot.

'You won't tell anyone?' he says now.

His lips are shiny from the food.

'I won't tell.'

In the car, when he's taking me home, he tells me he bought the wooden woman fair and square, but because of the 'business' with the *Angel*'s bell his collection must remain private.

'And I prefer it that way,' he says. 'There's something about Liberty that makes her hard to share. She's a pure survivor of the sea.'

'Why did you show her to me?' I ask.

He shrugs his shoulders and smiles. 'You have her breasts.'

He stops the car in front of my house and I get out. He speeds off.

When Davey comes home half an hour later I'm in bed with my seashore book.

'Did you win?' I ask by way of apology.

'Nah, the bastards trounced us. So you got home safe?' he asks by way of apology.

'Yeah. Yeah, I did.'

He doesn't say anything for a minute. He scans my face, as if something unfamiliar about it has caught his eye.

'What is it?' I ask.

'Oh ... nothing,' he says.

'Go and clean your teeth,' I say, 'your breath stinks of beer.'

I don't tell him about Bim's expensive car.

CHAPTER TEN

UPSIDE DOWN

Typical weekend. Davey's gone fishing with the boys, they've been going out quite regularly now it's October and the weather's warmer. I've done the cleaning. And I'm bored. I'm flicking through the pages of a magazine, checking the fashions, trouble is they're mostly skimpy and on the bodies of movie stars who are attending opening nights, not local history meetings. Those gossipy captions always read, 'So-and so, on the arm of her new lover'. Stars and royals, as bold as brass, they go round having one affair after another. It doesn't seem to worry them. It doesn't seem to cause them too much harm.

I asked Viv the other day and she said, yes, she'd had the odd entanglement. She was so nonchalant about it. Then I said, what about Ray? That's different, she said, and if she ever found out he'd been mucking around she'd take her faithful fruit knife to his unfaithful balls.

'But how is it different?' I said.

Viv looked incredulous, 'I know what I'm doing. He'd get carried away.'

Viv is confusing sometimes.

I get up, time to shake off the moony sort of mood

that's clung to me all day. I need a down-to-earth dose of Rosie Lunt.

When I get to Rosie's house she greets me at the door saying, 'Come on in if you must, love, but the place is a mess. I'm doing up me jams.'

She's got an old ringbinder book laid open on top of the dishrack. The paper is lined with thinnest blue, fading latitudes, yet they support a powerful scrawl, handwriting in ink so thick it could be tar. It's Rosie's mother's recipe for jam, come originally from across continents, now used with Coolie fruit, stewed and saturated through with sugar milled from Queensland cane. Rosie says, of course, she knows it off by heart but she likes to have it out for company.

'Rosie,' I say as I settle myself into her little kitchen, 'do you read the women's magazines?'

'Oh yairs,' she says. 'I like to keep up with the news.'

'You know those models and celebrities having all those love affairs? Imagine how much they'd get to learn about life and the world – every new partner would teach them something.'

'So that's what they're doing,' coughs Rosie. 'Night school.'

She puts a dollop of marmalade onto a saucer, blows onto it, then tips the plate this way and that. It's too runny still. She stirs the big pot of bubbling peel and returns to perch on the stool. I'm on the other side of the bench and feel like I'm talking to her through a slit since there's overhead cupboards above and the bench in front is covered with spotless glass jars lined up for the jam.

'You gotta be patient and you gotta watch out,' she says. 'The minute your back's turned the marmalade turns too and you're left with stodge.'

I can't put my cup of tea down. There's no room on the bench.

'You can't spoil it with too much testing. It's not like jelly.'

I've heard Rosie on the subject of jelly before. She's got a superstition about letting it set. She says if you keep wobbling it, the sugars evaporate and it turns bland, but far worse than that, your lack of discipline shows you'll probably die of a weak spleen. Rosie cooks with a complicated set of rules.

I balance the cup on my knee.

'Rosie, you were married for a long time.'

'My oath I was.'

I'm looking at her across the rows of jars.

'Were you happy?'

'No.'

'Not ever happy?'

'Royce never appreciated me.'

'Husbands never appreciate wives.' Everybody knows that.

'Except your father,' says Rosie. 'I used to look at the way your father loved your mother and wish Royce felt a pinch of that for me.'

'Did you ever …?'

'What?'

'Fool round?'

'No.'

'Did he ever …?'

'No,' she says, but she looks shifty.

'Never?'

'Don't scratch the surface.'

She gets up and returns to the boiler.

'Royce was not my cup of tea but he stuck by me.'

'Is that meant to be enough?' I say, more to myself, wondering. 'It doesn't seem much.'

'It's a lot.'

I'm turning the teacup round and round on the saucer, watching the brown dregs swill the leaves.

'What are you up to?' says Rosie, and when I look up she's eyeing me narrowly. 'Don't be a fool, Lal.' She's cross and she stabs the spoon back into the pot.

'Oh come on, Rosie, don't get snaky. What about adventure? And what about love? There's such a thing as love, don't you know?'

'Ah, wake up, girl.' She swipes a tea towel from the bench and wipes her hands and balls it up and throws it in the sink, 'You want to know what I know? You're a fool.'

She stands in her patch of kitchen, feet planted. She puffs up her chest.

'What I know?' she says. 'I know that when I was fifteen some young men got me and took me to some bushes and forced themselves on me. Do you understand what I'm saying?'

Her face goes hard, set.

'Royce saved me. He was the last one to get on but he stayed when the other two left and he helped me collect my things. He didn't discard me. Later, he called on me and was received by my parents, so that was something. Some girls in those days didn't end up as good as me. I never done the dirty on Royce, I put up with Royce, because he stuck by me. What I know is that something is better than nothing. When you grow up you have to face facts. Hand me that jar.'

At home.

Where's your mother when you need her?

My tea's gone cold.

The milk separates.

Water was never meant to go with fat.

I'm sorry, Rosie, that Royce and those boys left you with only facts. I'm sorry, but I was only dreaming and surely there's no harm in dreaming. It's all theoretical because, really, who would look at me?

Rosie wants me to face facts.

A blue tattoo of biro grows over the page, menacing the small print of the beginnings of a shopping list.

Dear Mum,

Rosie says something's better than nothing.

Well, what about Dad and I? Didn't we even rate that high – at the very least – weren't we your something?

How dare you think so little of us.

Who the hell were you, to think so little of us?

I am in Dad's house. I am turning it upside down, opening cupboards and pulling out drawers. I am a thief, a robber, a vandal. I'm dancing mad, turning from one thing to the next, upending order, shredding it. I am surrounded by shoes and skirts, bottles of oils and creams, belts uncoiled like striking snakes, scarves and handbags scattered. There's a straw hat with a flattened raffia flower and a green beret with its pumpkin stalk. Rugs and jumpers ripped out of the camphorwood box cough out the old-book smell of wool. Tartan skirt, country and western checked shirt, hibiscus flowers splashed across a dress or dressing-gown, I don't know which, it's just cloth I don't remember tossed onto other junk. Beads, earrings (all screwbacks); christening bangles, hers and mine; bracelet of charms, windmill, slipper, crown; a broken purse, the lining torn, a sixpence minted 1952.

And his stuff makes me sick.

He has it neatly folded and compressed into half drawers, the smallest nooks are his. He's shrunk himself, there's no space left for him – she's got it all.

I'm thorough, even lifting the waxed-paper linings of the drawers. I notice a nylon petticoat, underwear, see the rotting stitches in the falling hem of a black cocktail dress – what did she want with that? I have a sudden memory of her watch. But, of course, it's not there. She loved its luminous green hands, green numerals and date, loved that unearthly glow, because it reminded her of the night we waded in phosphorescence.

As much as I upend these ordered things there are no clues. Only clothes and a few old cosmetics. Where are the other things to say who she was? Papers to prove it.

The sideboard: plates for best, the bottom ones never used; linen serviettes in plush red; knives and forks mixed up with splayds, little plastic horse bedded down with the spoons. Birthday cards for her, for him, for me, all from her brother, 'all the best', is all he says over and over again. Candlesticks and candles with black wicks and warted wax.

The china cabinet: the door yawns open and drifts until it bangs the wall. A Bo Peep statue and a blue painted cat taken from their cold shelf feel carpet for the first time in years. Make way. I shove my fist down the deep throat of a large vase and find two buttons. Yellow and red.

The kitchen drawer, third one down: three egg rings, Yates sweet pea seeds, an apron with an ink blot where a pen's leaked, and a yellowed recipe cut out with pinking shears – Greek Roast Lamb.

The linen press: sheets, pillowcases (cotton and flannelette), towels she wrapped round me when I was a baby, a cheap box of mauve writing paper, tennis racquets, extension cords.

Laundry, the cupboard with the ironing board and vacuum cleaner in it: Dad's greatcoat.

That's it. There's nowhere else to look. But behind the sleeve of the big coat there's a showing of fawn gaberdine. It's her raincoat. I take it from the hanger. It's stiff with the starch of old sea breezes. In the pocket there's a gold hairclip, one of a pair she used to wear – I gave them to her. Sometimes I rearranged them in her honey-coloured hair making different styles while she laughed into the mirror. I put it to my nose now hoping to smell her. Nothing. Just the damp-clamping musk of salt. I check a second pocket for the other clip, but it's not there. Lost. Forgotten. Not even worth keeping track of. In its stead is the fragile head of a pussy willow. They grow in the dunes down at the beach and there's the odd clump sprouting by the inlet. They are the no-colour of rained-on sand. And they're soft.

Dad comes through the front door. I hear him going from room to room. It's a matter of time before he finds me here on the back step. I've got the gaberdine coat over my knees and the pussy willow in my hand. I'm crying.

'Are you alright? Who did this?' he says and his eyes are startled, shifting here and there.

'I did.'

His shoulders sag, he rubs his head.

Finally, he asks, 'What were you looking for?'

'I don't know,' I say.

Together, we put the things back. He's not telling and I'm not asking. Again. He knows where everything goes. In the kitchen, holding up the packet of sweet peas, he says, 'I think I'll plant these,' and puts them back in the drawer.

'They're too old,' I say.

'Sweet peas are lovely,' says he.

In the hallway his knees crack as he bends to pick up Bo Peep and the blue cat. He's about to put each one back exactly on its little dust-free spot when I stop him.

'It's okay, Dad, I'd better wipe in there.'

He nods but I don't think he likes losing their places.

The bedroom is the worst. We perch on the edge of the bed, shifting things to make room. Dad picks up a pointy-toed shoe with a mushroom heel. He's looking around the room but all the time his fingers feel for small parts of wear in the slope of the heel and the creases of the upper. Inside the shoe, his thumb comes to rest in the smooth dark dent made by the ball of her foot. He was her husband, he must have some clue as to why she left, but I know now if I asked him a direct question he would turn to ash, just exactly enough ash to fill Mum's shoe. He stares into the one empty corner of floor space.

'It's a mess,' he says.

We thought she was coming back.

I was a child, I didn't know you had to clear things out when people left or died. Anyway, we thought she was coming back. I didn't know to supervise him. When I moved out and married Davey I skipped that part. I just supposed he'd do it.

She was there in the way the furniture was arranged and the pictures were hung but I took that for granted because it was my home and had always been that way and Dad had never changed it. But I'd never thought to do an inventory of her. I didn't think there'd be so much or so little of her left.

Before I leave Dad's house I stuff Mum's hairclip into the prickly deep inside pocket of Dad's greatcoat and bury it there.

I'm done waiting. I give up.

CHAPTER ELEVEN
OLD MAN BREAM

I'm waiting for the fish. Staring hard at the spot in the water where my line pierces through and splits off at a strange angle. Again, the fish comes. Might be an old man bream, big and wise and cautious. I try not to think too much about the fish. Just keep my finger on the line, ready, and my eyes narrowed, glazed with concentration and the green glare off the water. Don't want to travel down the steep angle of line, don't want to think about the muddy flash of silver down there, in the dark, as the big bream turns to return to the bait. I don't want to think about the days and nights it's sped fast as an arrowhead through crusty corridors of oysters, or how it might have paused to spin its fins to hold station against strong currents, nibbling spat. I'm staying on my side and it's just my finger that's waiting for the tug to tell it what to do. We'll meet, the fish and I, if and when its back first breaks the water, and when adrenaline rings in my blood I'll let my arms and instinct do whatever they do. How big, how strong is this brute.

And if he flaps thickly on the worn timbers of the wharf he'll be on my side.

I'll admire him quickly. Before I put him, headfirst, into

the sugarbag. It can only be quickly. If I look too long I'll let him go.

I'm on my own.

CHAPTER TWELVE
THE PARTY

I'm taking off my party make-up now, wiping away mascara and staring into the bathroom mirror, wondering how I let it happen. We went to a party tonight for the Historical Society and during the speeches I rated a mention as the year's new member. Dr Ranold piped up, 'She's so quiet you wouldn't know she's there!' Suddenly they're all voting it my turn to give a talk at the next meeting. Democracy has its flaws. They reckon they take it in turns to research and present a topic of local historical interest from time to time but so far I haven't seen anyone else do it.

The black eyeliner smears in my eye socket and I look like a drug addict. More cleanser.

It was a weird night. When we got there Barbara Audette was doing her best to be a gracious hostess as she circulated among the members dotted round her living room, but a certain strain was already beginning to show. Imagine Snow White meeting all seven dwarfs for the first time and finding them totally unappealing.

'Oh yes, terribly lucky,' she'd said, passing a plate of smoked salmon scraps on little squares of peaty bread. She smiled with Colgate teeth and might really have looked very lucky except for the glassy glint of steel in her eyes.

I did not take the salmon, I wouldn't blame her if she hadn't been able to help herself. 'Nineteen Die in Fish Tragedy', the paper might scream tomorrow. At least there'd be two of us to read about it.

'Have another,' she said to Iris Marchant who elbowed Bertie to dig in while the good stuff was on offer.

'We are fortunate,' she continued, 'because there's precious little buildable land up here at the Heights. As it was the architect nearly gave himself a topographic hernia with this site. Bim insisted it was possible and, of course, since we're all here tonight, he was right.'

Mr Marshall swapped his champagne glass for another that was full on the table.

'Get it into ya, Mr Marshall,' said Davey, raising his can of beer in a here's cheers salute.

Davey had been sulky about coming when I asked him. He'd said, 'But it's only just November. You can't have a Christmas party in November.'

'Well there're only so many days in December,' I'd said. 'I suppose they're busy and they've got to start early.'

'Maybe they're so busy they're still running late from last year,' he'd said.

'So I am lucky to be living here,' Barbara simpered on.

'Position, position! Isn't that what they say?' said Bertie with his mouth full.

'Don't be disgusting,' snapped Iris and she stepped in front of him as if to cover him up.

Round swirled the hors d'oeuvres, strange things passed at nose level, pinwheels of cold rice wrapped with leaf, rolled-up slivers of meat.

'Emu,' whispered someone.

'Sushi,' corrected Barbara.

'Bless you,' said Davey and he got his hanky out of his pocket and offered it to her.

She stared at the neatly folded square on offer, at the navy-blue stitches of the machine-embroidered D. And then she turned, put the plate down on the glass-topped table, and walked away.

'When are they going to serve up the proper dinner,' he said.

'There might not be any.'

'What?'

'Have another beer.'

'I'm up to my stinking eyeballs and I'm still not pissed. They've put something in it.'

I parked him with Owen and Gaynor and a dapper Mr Hope, who I'd never met before. Mr Hope was saying he'd just recovered from the measles. I drifted away but not before I heard Davey say, 'Shit, mate, how are you? Doesn't that do something terrible to your balls?'

I looked over my shoulder to see how Mr Hope was coping. Not well. He was bright red and had dropped his olive onto the carpet.

At the bar Bim was pouring drinks. He looked smart in a beautiful pale-blue shirt and a pair of fawn trousers.

'Is Mr Hope another new member?' I asked.

'Alex?' he said. 'No – thank God,' and he pulled a face. 'He's Barbara's father.'

Bim and I stepped out onto a side balcony and the party rhubarb turned down a notch. A bit of the strained atmosphere from inside escaped out with us. We leant against the balcony rail. Bim leaned quite close. Far below we could see the white collars of breaking waves but the air was moist with a thick salt mist and the sound of the surf travelled up slowly to us, delayed.

I made a lame attempt at conversation, saying how what we hear doesn't always match what we see, especially at night, when we're more easily deceived.

He listened and he sort of looked at me sideways, appraising me, and he said, 'You always notice the little things that other people take for granted.'

I laughed and said I didn't think it was a skill, it was probably just my way of alleviating boredom.

'I don't believe in boredom,' said Bim.

He told me the last time he was bored was when he was fourteen and poor and at a loose end after the football season. In the holidays he caught the bus from Coolie to Pocket and walked along the beach staring at the reef off Black Angel Cove, like he was looking for a sign. 'I was jealous of Girlie,' he said, 'I wanted to be a hero too. We didn't have anything much else to distinguish us as a family and Girlie was always exhorting me to be brave like her and make her proud when I grew up. I was sweating on discovering my own destiny.'

'And did you?' I asked.

He smiled, 'It took a bit longer. I must've made a thousand footprints in the sand but after all the walking I did that summer the only thing I discovered was that the big toe of my right foot made a deeper impression than the left.'

I liked knowing that about his toes.

'He's not jealous of Girlie anymore,' chipped in Barbara from the dark.

We jumped a little. Her voice was brittle. She'd been there the whole time. She was sitting in a chair, well back in the corner. It was some sort of mod fifties-style sun chair that put its elbows up and wrapped itself round her. She'd kicked her shoes off and had her legs tucked up in the lap of the chair. She fumbled for cigarettes.

'Of course I'm not jealous now,' said Bim smoothly, turning to face her. 'I honour her memory. She made me what I am.'

'In more ways than one,' said Barbara bitterly. She lit her cigarette and then breathed out a long stream of smoke. 'You're so corny, Bim – the Flower of the Storm. When will we ever hear the end of her? Giving up her place in the lifeboat – which sank anyway – and surfing in on a bit of wreckage. A regular little Gidget, wasn't she?'

'Shut up, Barbara,' said Bim.

He wasn't angry but she kept going on, she called him Storm Boy, 'You didn't mind riding on her coat-tails when the fans named you that, did you, Bim? And once you were on you couldn't get off.'

'Leave it alone,' said Bim.

'You swallowed the whole cock and bull. Girlie Tyler – the great survivor!'

'Shut up,' he said again and he turned on her. 'She was nineteen. Only nineteen years old. Just a kid.'

They fell silent.

A lazy wave boomed up from below and a light went off in one of the houses strung along the scarp. Hands clasped, Bim leaned his forearms on the balcony rail and stared into the night. He scanned the beach, the dark sea, as if looking for more survivors.

Mr Marshall poked his head out through the doorway, he pushed his specs back up his nose, 'Thought I'd come out for some air,' he said, brandishing his champagne glass at a dangerous angle and slopping some of the contents.

'There's a lot of air out here, Mr Marshall,' said Barbara, 'but would you be a pet and get me another drink?'

'Let me,' I piped up, 'I need one myself.'

Bim started to move after me.

'Lovely,' said Barbara, 'because then Bim can turn his attention to Mr Marshall and entertain us with further details of Girlie's extraordinary and very long life.'

Getting back into the hubbub of the living room was a relief. Except it wasn't a relief for long.

Davey was holding court on one of his favourite themes – the Bush Fire Brigade.

'I wouldn't leave my house,' he was saying. 'I would not leave my house to those incompetent bastards.'

Alf nodded in agreement but Owen looked rankled, he probably had mates in the brigade. Davey twisted the lid off another stubby.

'They'd be out the front in a truck, full of the surprise of their own voices on the two-way radio, and meanwhile my mongrel house burns to the ground.'

It seemed as if the beer had a kick in it after all. I couldn't deal with it. I looked round for someone else to talk to.

Shona and Rhonda seemed safe. Their husbands had their heads together literally talking about the price of fish since their livelihoods depend on it – one's a marine engine mechanic and the other's in refrigerated freight. The girls were gossiping and I let it wash over me, didn't really listen, until the subject turned to Barbara Audette. Shona said she'd heard that Barbara goes on midnight shopping expeditions. As a cure for insomnia. Before she continued, Shona popped up on her tiptoes and made her head a periscope above the party crowd to check on Barbara's whereabouts. Bobbed back down with the all clear. Barbara drives for miles, apparently, all the way to Sydney in the dead of night – to window-shop. And she got booked once for jumping the gutter in the BMW and driving along the footpaths at the exclusive end of town. Even had the cheek to poke the nose of the car into the Louis Vuitton window, headlights on high beam to illuminate the luggage at the back of the shop. The police thought she was part of a ram raid. She told them she was just shopping and it was too damn cold to get out of the car.

'What with the fine and everything,' said Rhonda, incredulous, 'wouldn't you think she'd be better off with sleeping pills?'

Just in time I spotted Mr Hope coming our way and, nudging Rhonda to button up, I stepped out and pulled him into our orbit to make the formal introductions. Shona pumped him for information using the giggly-sweet technique, how long was he visiting, oh such a short stay, how nice, a property in the Hunter Valley.

'I see you've met my father.'

Barbara turned up beside us.

'Don't you think you ought to rest, my dear,' said Mr Hope, putting his arm round his daughter.

'I'm fully recovered, Daddy, though Lal did promise earlier to save my legs and fetch a drink. Didn't you, Lal?'

She hid the command in the arched span of her eyebrows.

Eels can get out of their pools and walk, I am told, when the water turns not to their taste.

Barbara shadowed me.

When there were no clean glasses left on top of the bar Barbara told me to look in the cupboard below. I resurfaced with a whiskey tumbler and a wedding photo. Her and Bim. Pushed to the back of the cupboard. They looked like they were in a snow dome, confetti falling, Barbara's white veil full of it, Bim's broad mountain shoulders capped with drifts of it, paper blessings. Barbara as beautiful as a movie star. Bim with a broken nose.

'Never get married in the middle of the football season,' she said, peering over my shoulder. They looked happy. Too happy to have to stay in the back of the cupboard now.

'How did you meet?' I asked her.

'You think us an unlikely pair? The broken-nosed footballer and the socialite?' she asked back.

I shrugged my shoulders.

'He gate crashed a party,' she said. 'A university party, that's where I met him. Yes, I was a socialite, Daddy had bags of money, but I was also – more so – a student. I fancied archaeology and dead languages.' She laughed. 'Not terribly useful. That night, Bim looked like a centurion freshly washed and newly returned to Rome after a hard war. He was ... acquisitive ... and hard to resist. He took me away from the party and later the university. I was in love and I allowed myself to be collected.'

Barbara sipped her drink and stared into the photo at her own youthful face.

'I regret the loss of those dusty tongues,' she said.

And that's when the hullabaloo started with the speeches and I got bulldozed into having to make a presentation at the next meeting. Dr Ranold, thanking the hosts, talked on and on and Bim came by with a bottle, topping up glasses for a final toast. He said sympathetically, but also with a wry smile, 'Now you're forced out of your comfort zone.' He filled my champagne flute and the liquid fizzed, threatening to spill, but at the last minute he gave the bottle an expert twist and he said, quietly, so that no one else could have heard, 'It can be exciting, taking risks. How brave are you?'

The last of my party face comes off onto the cotton pad. My public, not-tested-on-animals face is now a pink-grey smear of muck. The face that's left, the one that hangs in the mirror looking back – whose is that? And how could it command an audience? Let alone an audience of one?

I get myself to bed and dream of Barbara Audette sneaking down dark streets in her sleek car. But she's not window shopping – she's hunting for cats. There are lots of them skittering across the roads and they're all called Christine. She turns the wheel deliberately to run them down.

CHAPTER THIRTEEN

A GOOD IDEA

There's a little dead-end corner off the Reference section of the library labelled Local History. The Vampire Bride sits at one of the three small tables by the window. She has a needle and thread in her hands and her work is tilted towards the natural light. She might be repairing a book of the dead or stitching up spells. She looks up as I enter. Today she's wearing a purple velvet dress. Her eye shadow is painted in purple and red waves like a storm sunset. Black lipstick. A sharp ruby nose stud winks back a sting of light.

'Shit,' she says and sucks her finger.

It's her little finger and round it she wears a child's gold ring with a small flat heart stamped on it. Despite the needle wound she seems peaceful, happy at her task in a wash of sunlight.

I don't want to disturb her. By the look of her eyes she could do with a rest. I creep around having a look at what's what. I've never bothered to look in here closely. From a distance it looked boring. And after a quick circuit I can confirm it. This is a shame since you always hope your expectations will be reversed. It's a double shame because how am I going to concoct an interesting talk out of rate books. There're loads of them and hardly anything else.

I slump to a seat by a study carrel. There are rows of tomes gold-stamped *Royal Australian Historical Society – Journal and Proceedings*, there're electoral rolls, books with cuttings about the council, development plans and proposals. On a display stand on top of a catalogue there's a study entitled *Profile of Pedestrian Casualties in Coolie, 1977–88*.

This is terrible. I've rushed in here as soon as I could after the party to give myself maximum time to prepare, but how am I going to impress anyone with this material?

Maybe I could get a doctor's certificate. Except I'd have to get it from a doctor in Coolie. Couldn't ask Ranold.

'You alright?'

It's the Vampire Bride standing over me. Gives me a fright.

'You look like you're about to neck yourself.'

It's an option I hadn't thought about.

I begin to confide in the Vampire Bride and I'm so anxious about my predicament that I don't realise how rude I'm being, slagging off at her library. I forget to be scared of her.

'Look at that!' I say, waving towards the pedestrian casualties report.

'Yeah,' she says, deadpan. 'Might be m'best so far. I'm having a competition with myself. To create the most boring display. The one on pest control in public buildings had a lot going for it.'

'Sounds too interesting,' I say.

Her doom face splits a little with what might almost be a crooked smile.

'I'm trying to wake up the other librarians but they're

fucken comatose. They stick me off down here to keep me out of the way but it's a mistake. Because I've seen their neglect.'

She's getting worked up and she's jabbing that needle and thread round and I lean back in case she makes a mistake and stitches up my nose. I'm getting nervous of her again.

'See that!' and she pigsticks the needle towards a locked glass cabinet with a small brown box inside on an otherwise empty shelf. 'That represents this library's total collection of personal papers, oh and there's one audio cassette tape with a recording of one oral history. The woman in charge of acquisitions oughta be shot!'

The Vampire Bride would not look out of place with a revolver in her hand. She slumps into a chair too.

'What are you mending?' I ask. 'An old atlas?'

'Pah,' her black lips twist. 'Another rate book.'

Now we're both glum. No, I'm glum and the Vampire Bride is sullen with some thunder rolled up in her brow.

We are like this, quiet and almost companionable, when in crashes a whirling dervish of a woman. She's talking so fast her hands have trouble keeping up, her words and sentences rush on, she fires them out in a Morse code staccato with the half sense of telegramese. Your brain has to do all these quick little pole vaults to leap the gaps and peg in meanings in between.

'You wouldn't read about it,' she says, '… well in a library you might,' (gongs of laughter), '… and then he said, "get over … an emergency"… you know what they're like … "I need to know" … yelling and swearing … "pronto"… if I tell mother … won't vote again … zoning by-laws 1962.'

The Vampire Bride and I look at each other. It's the mayor's secretary and she's run over from the chambers next door. It doesn't help that she's out of breath. Her lime-green skirt flirts round the room, her bangles clack.

'Absolute … livid … "Industrial!" … I say it can't be, he says … "not be, the bastard" … yearbook 1962.'

'We don't have it,' comes the Bride's calm voice.

I'm about to point to the shelf holding all the council records when the Bride throws me a look with an edge forged in Toledo as she worms over and casually stands in front of them.

'Joking … you're …'

'Afraid not,' says the Bride. 'Lost that book in the great fire of '85. There're a few crucial years missing.'

'But … his head … flip open.'

'Just one of the many acquisitions we need to make for this section.'

'Our own files … shocking mess … nothing for it … search or … oh my God … chopping block.'

And off she twirls.

'Budget increase … do nicely,' shouts the Bride after her. And then she turns to the shelf and slides out the 1962 yearbook and walks very deliberately, almost with a wedding march step, over to the window and chucks it out into the garden.

'You've done me a big favour,' I say. 'You've given me a good idea.'

One week later the Bride is sitting in my car saying, 'What is this fucken place? Is this it, or are we getting petrol?'

I drive the ute in through the open gates of the Auto Acre.

'They hold the meetings in the lunch room here. Bim Audette's the president.'

'Christ, you chat away as nice as a piece of apple pie right in the middle of a car graveyard?'

The wrecks stretch away to our right, rows of twisted metal. Chrome and ducos of different hues all mangled together. The heaps glint under the scrupulous spread of floodlights. Christine's cat gang patrols the alleys.

'Look!' says the Vampire Bride, charged suddenly by a stab of excitement. 'There's the front half of a Valiant Regal. Kenny would be stoked. He makes sculptures from things like that.'

Kenny is the Bride's boyfriend and I hope Davey never finds out and decides to start collecting modern art.

Usually I try to ignore the wrecking yard as I drive in – all those cars. What about all their drivers, there could be human body parts in there as well. Quick smears of snatched lives. Avoid the flash picture – pieces of my mother. It could have happened.

'They do repairs here too,' I say, waving left towards the panel beating area and the paint shop and the parts division.

'He owns all this?'

'He's rich,' I say, and I glide in, parking next to Owen's Landcruiser.

We're a bit late. When I went to pick her up I waited in the car for ages. The Bride could only find one of her black net gloves. Since they are fingerless and not made for warmth I couldn't really see the worry if one whole hand was missing. But she obviously wanted to make a good impression. And I suppose librarians have it in them to prefer organisation and symmetry.

The exterior of the Auto Acre might be well lit but the inside of the lunch room is blinding. If light had an equivalent to sound you'd be standing in the middle of a trumpet blare. We sit in the darkened cab of the ute for a minute. I'm nervous.

Everyone else is already there. Full house. Behind the glass sliding doors they are positioned round a central table like a tableau of the Last Supper. Owen is leaning over Treasurer Bertie's shoulder confusing him with change for a raffle ticket, the little grey cash box open in front of them; Mr Marshall and Gaynor Daley are bent to the minutes book, it's as thick and impressive as a set of scriptures; Shona and Rhonda have balls of wool out and Shona's demonstrating a crochet stitch with the MacDonald sisters looking on; Bim is pouring Alf and Dr Ranold a cup of tea from the big silver pot but he's spilt some on the table which Iris Marchant is wiping up (she's got a Tupperware container with water in it and she wrings out the tea-stained cloth with the disgust and vigour you'd reserve for choking a rat); and coming towards the table from the kitchenette, bearing a plate of biscuits so proudly you'd think it was a turkey dinner, is Janet Constable.

'Come on,' says the Bride. 'They can't eat you.'

As she gets out of the car in her black knit top and her black tulle skirt, and her purple-stockinged legs with the rose motif pocked on them, with her boots laced up over the bone bolts of her skinny ankles, I realise I've been selfish to worry about myself. I'll only be the entrée.

'So glad ewe could join us,' says Janet. 'And how nice,

ewe've brought along a little friend.'

The official part of the meeting is rattled through out of deference to the guest. None of them were concentrating too much on the proceedings anyway; even Gaynor, the pretend hippie, was looking the Vampire Bride up and down and Bertie's eyes were hanging out on stalks until Iris rapped a teaspoon over his knuckles.

I push back my chair to stand up and begin my talk and it makes a noise. My bra's too tight. My toenails are too long in my shoes. My voice has a quaver in it.

'I would like to call my talk "People Versus Pest Control", or, "The History of the Future".'

I look up. When I was practising at home Davey told me to look up. That's what the speakers at the Lions Club do, he says. They keep looking up from notes written on little cards. I wish I hadn't followed his advice. The members' faces are blank, all except Bim's, and his has that eyebrow-raised, half-smile look. The Bride is sprawled in her chair staring at the floor. In my despair I shuffle the cards up by mistake. Oh God, I'll have to wing it.

'My horror ... er ... imagine my horror when I went to the library to do some research for this talk and ... ah ... there was nothing there. I mean, the library was there, there just wasn't anything else there. Except my friend, who I met. She's a librarian and she's going to talk in a minute but she made me see something very important. She made me see that history is about people, not buildings or pedestrian crossings.'

They're trying so hard to understand my gobbledygook that they all wear an identical expression, noses and foreheads pinched as if poised for a collective sneeze. In practice sessions Davey made me slap my fist into my palm to emphasise the main points. I do it now. 'Not buildings or pedestrian crossings.'

I sit down.

The Bride looks over to me as if to say, is that it? You've caved in already? And she climbs out of her chair and her lethargy to take the floor. She frowns at the ceiling for a moment, then begins.

'It's like this. The Local History Section of the Coolie library is a joke. It's a repository for council records. If you want to know stuff about the history of petty bureaucracy you're well served, but what about the history of the people. Where are the letters and diaries and photographs of the ordinary people? Where are their voices and stories preserved? Don't bother looking because they're not there. The history of the everyday hasn't been collected and archived – not just because the fascists in control of the budget don't care – but because you don't care either. If you did, you'd be out there doing something about it. You'd be putting your biscuits back in the kitchen and getting about collecting stuff, asking friends to donate stuff, old family papers. You'd be borrowing a tape recorder and putting down some precious oral histories. If you want you can lobby the library board and the council until you're blue in the face but to really get something done you've gotta be prepared to take the lid off the compost bin yourselves and dig for the good stuff. You know what I mean. Get your hands dirty. Put your teapots and your knitting away. You're the Historical Society – you oughta be ashamed of your fucken selves.'

She sits down.

Everybody else stands up.

Pandemonium.

It was 'disgusting', it was 'brave', it was 'inspirational', it was 'insulting', there is clapping, there is sneering, there's a riot of reaction and the meeting is reopened and the members called to order, 'Order, ORDER! PLEASE!' says Bim Audette.

In a narrow vote it's decided that I will be responsible, in conjunction with the Vampire Bride as a representative of the Coolie library, for co-ordinating a community-wide appeal for historical material. All items are to be lodged with the library for cataloguing and preservation.

'I don't know,' says Shona, still looking shaky. 'We haven't actually done anything in years.'

Bim congratulates me. Me. I'm elated, I'm aerated, I've got lemonade in my blood. We have a cause.

Suggestions and arrangements are made and unmade, argued over. The Bride slaps a pamphlet on the table, saying, 'You'd better book in for this, and pronto.'

'I can't go to that,' I say.

'Yes you can.'

She wants me to go to a 'methodology' seminar about oral history, hosted by the Royal Australian Historical Society.

I complain, 'It's out of my league.'

'I suppose I could go … ' begins Bim – but the Bride cuts across him – 'Don't be pathetic, Lal. Muscle up.'

The evening breaks up much later than usual. Janet fusses with some cranky tidying up. 'Eleven p.m. and we didn't even cut the cake!' She shifts chairs and wipes round people.

Owen does the unimaginable and offers to take the Bride home and she accepts. Owen in his battle jacket and the Bride in her funeral parlour garb seem unlikely friends, but apparently he's managed to get her interested in plagues. Iris and Bertie round up Mr Marshall and the MacDonald sisters, looks like they're operating a bus service tonight. As they step out the door Iris confides to Mr Marshall that it's just as well the MacDonalds don't have one good ear between them what with all that filthy language flying about.

We are all noisy in the Five Wells night. Goodbyes and revving engines in the dewy Five Wells night. Bim locks up and walks me to the ute.

At the door of her white Daihatsu, Janet Constable is doing an elaborate thing with keys.

I get into the ute and Bim walks on to the gates.

Janet climbs into her car and fiddles with the rear-view mirror.

I turn on the ignition.

Janet winds down her window and makes a deferential signal with her hand, 'After you.'

Bim stands at the open gate.

I reverse out. Swing the wheel. Edge back to give her room.

She backs out, her face over her shoulder a ghastly white from the blast of my headlights. She pauses, maybe to put the car in gear, but then makes out she's having some awful tussle with the seat belt.

'You go on,' she waves me round.

Bim stands at the gate and watches me go. A small wave from the hip.

CHAPTER FOURTEEN

PORTRAITS

When I get to the Coolie library the Vampire Bride has her head stuck on the glass plate of the photo-copier with the lid closed down as far as it will go. She keeps her face still and reaches her finger round to the start button. A bright bar of green light moves under her.

'What are you doing?' I ask.

'Self-portraits,' she says, pulling her head out. 'I'm gonna put them in a card to Kenny.'

She fans out a selection for viewing. She's squished her face onto the glass and smeared her features this way and that, pulled her lips to show her gums, spread her nose, dragged an eyelid down, framed her face with her hands and moved her fingers at a critical time so the fingertips look four inches long.

'Which one's the best?' she asks. 'What about this one?'

It is a breast. It takes me a minute to work it out.

'Is it safe, doing that with a photocopier?'

'Bit like giving yourself a mammogram,' she says. 'I thought about, you know, going all the way – Kenny would appreciate it as a statement about art – but it'd be a bit hard to explain if I got caught out.'

'Yeah,' I say, 'I'm sure it would.'

I flip through the pages again. 'This one's nice.' She had her necklace, a chain with a cross, draped round her face and over her nose and pressed into her cheek.

'Too conservative. Anyway, the machine's warmed up. The head librarian's out at a meeting so the coast's clear.'

She folds up her self-portraits carefully and slips them between the covers of a big art book. She pauses at the breast.

'Maybe I should have gone all the way?' she says.

I hesitate. 'It could have been … awkward,' I say.

She nods ruefully and puts them all away.

'Look at this good paper I stole,' she says. 'Perfect.'

She's got two reams of copy paper and the outer wrapper of one is ripped open to expose a slash of royal purple.

'Well, it's your favourite colour,' I say.

'Yeah, it is,' says the Bride as if her prejudice for purple were a surprise revealed.

'Here's the notice,' she says. 'If you want to change anything – tough. Took me ages to write.'

I look over it. It's pretty good.

HISTORICAL SOCIETY

'Those were the good old days' – or were they?
How will we know unless we start collecting the
evidence now?

The Pocket Head Historical Society invites
everyone in the local community to contribute to
the Shire archive in Coolie library by donating
family records, diaries, letters, photographs, or
any other items of interest. The library will
catalogue and preserve donated documents,
guaranteeing their survival as a valuable
community resource in the twenty-first century.

You can help now.

Historical Society members will also shortly begin
a programme of recording the voices and
memories of some of the long-time residents of
Pocket Head. Become a participant! If you've got
a story to tell, tell us!

To make a contribution or for more
information ring:
Lal ph: 4382 7949

We load up the machine and set it going.

'I reckon a thousand copies would be enough,' says the Bride.

We shut the door on the empty office area, leaving the photocopier to pump away, and stand guard outside trying to look as inconspicuous as possible. We wander over to the newspaper tables and perch on the high stools. It's a perfect vantage point. We turn the pages of a *Sydney Morning Herald* to make us being there seem natural but I can't relax. I'm cricking my neck trying to see if any of the staff are coming. We haven't done anything all that illegal but we have stolen public paper for private use and snitched some toner – even if it is for a good cause.

I whisper to the Bride, 'Don't you think we should've asked the library officially for their co-operation? We're doing all this stuff in the library's name.'

'Nah,' she whispers back unconcerned and more intent on studying the ads for the Sydney movie houses. 'They'd just make difficulties. This way, they're forced into it.'

I'm not convinced. I check for staff members again. 'They're gonna find out sooner or later and when they do they're not going to like it.'

'Later's better – oh, look, *La Strada* is playing. "Classic Italian cinema from the 1950s." I'd love to see that.'

I don't think I would mind if I missed it.

She turns more pages, skips over the classifieds to the sporting section. There's a big colour picture on the back page of a footballer, his leg at full stretch kicking for touch. 'King of League Signs New Deal', screams the headline.

'All that thigh,' ruminates the Bride. 'It's enough to put you off meat.'

She prefers her men scrawny. I've seen Kenny. He looks like he's recovering from something.

'I think it's sexy,' I say. 'Those thick strong legs – those little shorts.'

She laughs. 'So that's why you're attracted to Bim Audette!'

'What!' I say.

'I've seen the way you check him out. He's got the left-overs of those footballers' legs – he used to be a footballer.'

'Yeah, I know, everybody knows.'

She's getting wound up now, 'He was this district's greatest-ever export to the league.'

'I know.'

'Every time he even sneezed it was reported in the *Angel Advertiser*. Let's get out some old *Advertisers* and have a perve.'

She disappears. She's on the hunt for a youthful Bim Audette, pride of Coolie Shire, poor boy made good. She is tracking down his thighs. I feel a little squirm in that inside spot between my belly button and my pubic bone. It feels good.

The Vampire Bride turns the dry pages of the *Angel Advertiser* for me. They arc past. Her fingernails are black polished but scratched to patches like blood blisters and make me want to find a bucket of ice so she can rest her throbbing hands. But she keeps turning the pages.

'There! Bingo!' she says, and she stabs a damaged finger into the dark chest of Bim in a dinner suit receiving some award.

'Look at his hair, he was a good-looker when he had more hair.'

Out loud I agree with her, but, really, I don't mind the way it is now.

The photograph is one of several in a feature article on the life and times of the local hero after his two-hundred-and-fiftieth senior game. In the middle of the double-page spread there's an action shot. It's Bim, mud-spattered and straining, putting the ball down for a critical try to even up the score in a vital game. The caption reads, 'Storm Boy Issues Warning – Audette Never Says Die'.

The Bride is babbling on, '… you can see can see why he captured such attention, he wasn't afraid to seize the moment, was he? … Kind of majestic …'

Inexplicably, my mood flattens. I retreat from the Bride's voice into another picture, one with a fake torn edge made to look as if it had been ripped in a hurry from a family album. It doesn't make me feel any better. From among four rows of arms-crossed Coolie players stares the grey but recognisable face of a sixteen-year-old boy. It's a cold day in 1966. A list of names under the photo, bottom row, left to right, and in the centre, 'B.W. Audette (Captain)'. Yes. That's him. It's a different face, smooth, and serious with the importance of a premiership win, but the face the boy becomes is there too, lurking round the eyes and the set of his chin. Determination mixed with charm.

It's the face of a boy who'd look at a hundred other girls before he'd look at me.

CHAPTER FIFTEEN
PUTTING THEM AWAY

I'm at Dad's place. The late afternoon sun streams through the verandah windows, the mild temperature outside is magnified in here, and there's a bar of glare dividing the room between Dad and me which is handy – it keeps us in our respective corners.

I've just finished vacuuming his floor (he doesn't do it often enough for my liking), and I've started ironing. I thought it would please Dad if I did a quick clean through, but he seems miffed about me invading his territory and taking over. He's bickering with me, jousting, to regain ground, and now he's hit the jackpot, probing on a sensitive topic.

Sprawled in his armchair, he kicks at the Audettes' ironing basket, 'Isn't she any better yet?'

'Oh … yeah … she's okay.'

'Then how come you're still doing her ironing?' He half kicks the basket again as if it's distasteful and pushes it with the side of his outstretched foot to shove it further away.

'It's not much. Really. A few things once a fortnight.'

Bugger, I'm not doing a very good job. I'm rushing, I'm a little manic today, and I've just pressed a crease into the back of Barbara Audette's skirt.

'But she's alright?' he screws up his face.

As a foil, I hold up the skirt and give the crease an exaggerated frown, then bringing it closer to my face, I mumble behind its ocelot pattern, 'It's just that ... it's something that does take a long time to recover from and ... I can't tell her I'm stopping just yet ... it doesn't matter, don't worry about it, Dad.'

I glance at him quickly to see how that went down. He is unmoved. He looks like an old king in his seat in the burning sun; taking the light, his tousled grey hair is a fiery crown.

I realign the seams of the skirt and press again, briskly. That will have to do. I want this job done. I want everything in order before I go away, though I'll only be absent for an overnight. The Bride signed me up for that Royal Australian Historical Society lecture and it's on this Saturday. December the fourteenth. It's circled in black on my calendar. I'm not sure what I'm meant to do there – listen and maybe take notes?

Dad hasn't given up, he pokes his finger into the glare, 'I saw her at the shop the other day and she looked fine to me.'

Bim might be coming to the seminar, either him or Dr Ranold. Probably Ranold.

'She bought that stuff, cream cheese. There's nothing wrong with her. Isn't there someone else who could do with your help by now?'

I wish he'd stop. No way can I tell Dad that Barbara Audette has taken to leaving baskets of ironing on my back porch along with envelopes of money. Davey's not very impressed either. I return it to her done, embarrassed to think someone might see me skulking away from her front door having hung what I could on her Ali Baba pots but I never take the money, thinking surely she'll eventually get the message.

'What could be wrong with her? She looked perfectly well waltzing round on her two legs in that shop.'

'Yes, Dad.'

'Well what's wrong with her?'

'Nothing, Dad.'

'That's what I'm saying.'

I hang up the skirt and pick out a bunch of handkerchiefs, smooth them, get that iron flying, I want the job done, I'm rushing because I don't want to do this intimate thing for the Audettes anymore, I want to put them both aside, put them out of the way.

Dad says, 'It's not on. You should stand up for yourself, Lal.'

That's rich, coming from him.

I leave the ironing board and pull out a wad of Historical Society flyers from my bag. I say, 'Maybe you'd like to give me a hand and start folding these? When the Bride and I come to do our letterbox drop it'll be easier if they're folded.'

He grumbles about sheltered workshops and how there's no need for me to provide him with idiotic occupational therapy, he says he's already done a full day's work today at Nelson Purselle's digging out a dead mulberry tree.

'Please yourself,' I say, 'but it's just to help me.'

I drag the traymobile over towards his chair anyway, and put down the pile of purple papers, passing him one to read as I walk away, 'Is there anything you'd like to contribute?'

He looks at it.

I fill the iron up with a bit more water, it gurgles and hisses. I take up a shirt of Bim's.

'Anything, Dad?'

He stares into the sun.

'No,' he says.

'Not even any stories about when you were a boy?'

For a long time he doesn't reply and then he says, 'I was born old.'

'Mum used to say –'

'– I haven't got any stories to tell.'

'– She used to say you were energetic and optimistic as a young man and then you changed.'

'I had responsibilities. A wife and a child are precious and you have to look after them.'

Well I don't know what he was doing because he didn't do a very good job.

He says, 'That Audette woman is taking advantage of you.'

And then he tugs the traymobile closer and grabs a stack of the A4 papers and begins to fold, purple edge to purple edge and in half again. Hunched in his throne. After awhile he says emphatically into the dividing glare, 'I haven't got anything to contribute.'

I concentrate on the ironing. I clamp my nose and breathe out of my mouth to avoid the intoxicating smell of a man's body rising from warm clothes.

CHAPTER SIXTEEN

MOTEL EDEN

The man and the woman held hands but their fingers were thick and gammy. The lime-green neon tube wasn't thin enough to make a good job of fingers. Over their private parts were fig leaves which tick-tocked clockwise and back. The woman had her other hand outstretched and balanced on her open palm was an orange word, 'VACANCY'.

We pulled in. Our faces jaundiced as we passed under the sign. Bim stopped the car in front of the flywire door of the Reception at Eden's Motel.

We are not meant to be here. Of course.

At this very moment I'm meant to be in my cousin's lounge room in Top Ryde, listening to her talk above the noise of the television set and watching her step over the sprawled bodies of her children who only ever move to look past her legs when their view of the box is momentarily obscured. I'm meant to have my overnight bag parked on the end of the youngest's bed which is built to look like a fire engine.

Today we went to the city, Bim and I, to attend the seminar about gathering oral history. In the early evening they served wine and cheese in front of the open double doors of the lecture hall, and Bim, leaning casually against a table like a university student, said, 'Don't go to your cousin's tonight.'

I took a sip of the warm wine and to my surprise I said, 'Alright.'

And Bim? I don't know where Bim is meant to be but it's not here, not stepping out of Reception at Eden's Motel holding a key ring with a big wooden leaf attached.

We crawl along in the car past the already closed restaurant, past units 4, 5, and 6, follow the driveway round the back where the L shape of the building is revealed, and stop outside number 9. In front of unit 16 a commercial traveller repacks the back of his station wagon, juggling sample boxes, but otherwise there's nobody else about.

I didn't ask where we were going when we left the seminar but I was surprised when we ended up back on the freeway which led to the coast and home. It grew dark and the traffic was fast and the white lines slipped in a blur under the car when Bim changed lanes. He turned on the radio and old thin jazz came through the speakers. The music of American ghosts crackled in the smart interior of Bim's German car.

I wondered if my mother ever travelled like this, in a car like this, that ate the road.

Bim hands me the wooden leaf and says, 'You go in, I'll get us some dinner.'

I stare at it glumly and then I feel his fingers on my lips, his gentle pressure parts them and I feel all their pursed tension draining away and I know why I am here.

I don't know where he'll go to find food. We went two exits further than the Coolie off-ramp and pulled in just off

the freeway here where there's only a petrol station and
Eden's Motel, and a greyhound racing track, but it's not
dogs night – the joint's in darkness.

I turn the key in the door of number 9 and swing it open.
Snap on the bright light.

I am meant to be at Lorraine's, that's where I'm meant to
be right now, this instant, passing the bowl of chips and
raising my eyebrows and laughing when she tells me
Richard, her ex-husband, has taken up aerobics.

But I am not at Lorraine's. I rang and told her I was too
tired and got a lift home after all. But I am not at home
either. I am under this bright light – overexposed.

Jasmine and cooked fish and pillows on the bed flat as
tablets. This is my room of love.

I could shut the door but the breeze which brings in
these tangled smells also shifts the air and I can't kill it. I
could do something to make the place look not so stark.
I could toss my handbag on the bench along the wall and
let its contents scatter as a way of staking claim. I could
turn on the television set, boil up the jug, twist paintings on
the walls, go into the bathroom and turn on all the taps, nip
out to the petrol station and buy myself a packet of cigarettes, take off my clothes and wrap myself in motel towels,
even tuck my hair into a towelling topknot, and Bim could
find me, doing the drawback on an Alpine cigarette, and I
would own the room.

Instead, I take my jacket off and drape it over a corner of
the bed. I sit in the only chair. The jacket looks wrong.

Viv says you need new underwear if you're going to have
an affair. Black slippery stuff. But I'm frightened to put that
material too close to my body in case of fire.

Bim brings pizza and news of the outside world. He brings in the bags, and the papers from the seminar, and searches the cupboards for glasses and a corkscrew. No corkscrew. In the end he pushes the cork into the bottle with the handle of a spoon. We talk about wine, I don't like red wine, he's bought red wine, and when I taste it it's smooth and rich and I do like it. We talk about pizza, worst takeaways ever eaten, he wins with deep-fried lasagne, we laugh, we are having a good time. We eat, we are hungry, we eat until there are only scraps of capsicum and grease spots left in the bottom of the box. And then when the food is gone we run out of things to say.

He blows across the top of the wine bottle and makes a moon sound. It's a mistake. He tidied up the takeaway boxes and put the grease-smeared glasses on the telephone table and he took the wine bottle and put it to his lips. The moon sound. So hollow.

I go to the bench and get my handbag, do up the clasp.

'Don't,' he says, taking it from my shoulder.

The bed was dry land. An island in the middle of the room. All round it the carpet buckled in unsteady waves, the turquoise loom now knee high, now to the waist, now dropping away-o. We could not sink but neither could we stand. Our stomachs keeled. Gravity demands dry land.

Early morning.

I sit in my chair of the night before when I had studied the unsatisfactory fall of my jacket, but now I view Bim, lying in the wreckage of our exploded bed. He has ginger hairs curling on the backs of his legs. The rest of his body is covered by a tousled sheet and two pillows, so I've only these two legs for company while the majority of his body, under bedclothes, snores. They are white, these two legs. Like scissor blades. If I put my fingers to my ears to stop the rattle of his sinuses and the roar of freight trucks through the thin ply of the motel door I would surely hear the sea and Bim would seem something fragile, washed up to me.

And how does Davey sleep this early morning? Davey, you must stay two dimensional and thin for me, this early morning.

I go to the bathroom and find a glass wrapped in paper on a shelf behind the mirror. I take a long drink of water and then I clean my teeth. I lie back down in the narrow margin of bed and try to sleep.

We are woken some time later by a knocking which doesn't appear to be coming from the door. Bim leaps up and scouts along the front wall of the room looking for a vital clue and 'Ah ha!' he says when he finds it – the handle to a servery hatch. He drags in a tray of breakfast.

'I ordered last night,' he says. 'Didn't know what you might like so I asked for plenty.'

'A cup of tea,' I say.

He puts the tray on the floor beside the bed and pours from silver pots.

'Milk?'

He is nude. Nude but not naked. His is the body of a veteran sportsman clad in old scars and still-defined muscle and it's a body that is not afraid.

We sip companionably until I begin to trace the purple scar coiling round his left knee.

We do not eat the breakfast.

Rosie Lunt told me once that her husband Royce often pretended not to hear her – particularly if he didn't like what she had to say.

Just before I get in the shower, just, just before I've quite shut the door, I hear Bim take the telephone off the hook, a small click I didn't know I was hoping not to hear. It's the click of reality, the beginning of deceit. And isn't it somehow ironic that I've gone and done this whole Motel Eden thing only to have my existence denied? The shower drums. Steam swells and billows and I start to hum, trying to turn myself into a Royce, but I can still hear the slow return of the old dial, through the shower screen and the closed door. I would like to stop humming because just now I remember this is a tune my father used to sing on Saturday mornings. Mr Happy. Mr Optimistic Family Man. I turn the taps off and take a towel from the rail. It is too small and too often washed. I keep humming as I dress to give Bim privacy.

In Reception, when we go to pay, Bim fingers the scalloped edges of the postcards stacked in a display rack. He presses hard as if he'd welcome the bright snick of a paper cut but there is none. He turns the rack; girl with large beach ball flips past, crimson waratah, two kangaroos with cricket bats, then the rest a blur as Bim twirls the thing round and round, the Holiday Coast and all its pleasures just a murky blur. Creak, creak as the rack spins and the postcards flip forwards in their holders. Mr Eden, figuring the bill, glances up, then scurries back to the figures, making them leap across the pad in time to the creaking stand.

Back in Pocket Head Bim drops me off and I stand for a minute outside my run-down home, the overnight bag slung over my shoulder. I'm like a hitchhiker who, arriving at a familiar destination, is both relieved and disappointed to find the place seems just the same.

'Hello, love,' says Davey.

As I walk in the door I feel a sudden roundness between my legs in the place where another man's cock has been.

'How are you?' I say, heading for the kettle.

The roundness feels full and empty at the same time.

'Good,' he says.

A dull pang twangs high up in there where I am swollen and fluid. It's a throb of guilt, my body registering betrayal, but what shocks is that the ripples of that small contraction are also pink with lust. My anatomy is proud of what it's done.

'I would be good,' he says, preoccupied, 'if only … I could get this bloody wick to stay straight in the metho.'

He's seated at the kitchen table surrounded by small tools, Brasso and dust cloths, a water jug, methylated spirits and matches. He's tinkering, as he does once in a blue moon when he's bored, with the donkey engine his father gave him.

'Have a good time?' he says.

'Yeah. No. Yes and no.'

The dull pang comes again where I have been a circle round another man.

'How was the club?' I ask, plucking the old cold tea bags out of the teapot.

'Oh, it was a pretty good night. The boys went a bit out of control.'

He strikes a match and puts it to the wick which smokes before a little blue flame takes and turns orange. He slides the brass bowl holding the spirit into the gap under the boiler, his big fingers pushing gently to nudge it the last way in.

'I wasn't that pissed – didn't have the taste up. Went to bed, tucked myself in, slept like a top. Must have gone unconscious because when I woke up it took me a few minutes to work out why you weren't there.'

He smiles.

'Tea or coffee?' I ask.

'Surprise me.'

While I'm mucking about trying to find where Davey's put the sugar he lets out a cheer as a whisker of steam climbs out the funnel of the donkey engine. He puts a giant finger to the little flywheel and away it spins.

'There you go,' he says. 'The Industrial Revolution!'

'What?' I'm clinking cups together asking for clarification.

'It was as simple as that,' he says, pointing to the toy on the table with the dramatic flourish of a barrel girl. 'Just letting off steam changed the world!'

CHAPTER SEVENTEEN

DISTRIBUTING THE
PURPLE PAPER

We are distributing the purple Historical Society leaflet to launch our campaign. We are foot soldiers in what has turned out to be an unpopular cause. Bim said he might call by and his status and his charm sure would have helped, but he hasn't showed. I think I'm glad. I'm uncertain how I'll be in front of him or how he'll be in front of me. I don't know if I'll take one look at him and wonder why I did it, or if I'll feel another coil of lust come twisting out. I'd need some signal from him so I can follow the lead. To be honest, as well, I don't want to face being the blank he'd make me if he pretended that nothing had ever happened.

So it's good he hasn't showed.

The Bride and I started off doing a simple letterbox drop. We split up and I sent her down the Esplanade so I could avoid the Catholic church. I don't like going past it in December. They've got this box on the lawn, a wire grille over it, with a spotlight aimed in on Mary and Joseph and the shepherds and the three wise men and the baby Jesus. They need the wire because hooligans throw bottles at them but it doesn't seem right to keep them in a cage. They shouldn't be out in public round the clock, in all weathers. Every year as I avoid that street I tell myself to write to the Catholic church and ask them could they at least please just put their Holy Family safe inside at night. But I never do.

I don't think the Bride has any such worries because it didn't take her long to knock over the Esplanade and come and help me. She's certainly no dawdler. She has a quick furtive air and she shoved her flyers in and flipped down the lids of the letterboxes with a hastiness which implied imminent detonation. You could see venetian blinds snap open then shut in the windows of the houses on her side of the street. Noses appeared at front doors, heels stuttered down front paths to see what she'd delivered. Some of the flyers were scrunched up without even being looked at.

We decided to try a more personal approach and give doorknocking a go but that didn't go well either. Witness our failure with Margaret Berg. She opened her door just wide enough to stick her head out. You know the way a magpie turns its face, now left then right, its beak the axis of its stare, well, she did that to us. It didn't take her long to decide the Bride was a poisonous worm. I had hardly started our spiel before she interrupted and attacked her, 'You're not from round here.'

'We're collecting material for the library,' I began again. 'Papers, photos, things that might be of historical interest. So we've got some record of what everyday life was like when you were a girl, what it was like for you and your family.'

Margaret's round brown eye fixed on mine. I could see her thinking, 'You might be sucked in, Lal, but I'm not fooled.' You could tell she thought the Bride was a drug addict casing the joint, while only pretending to do a community good deed.

'It's no good,' I said to the Vampire Bride when we retreated to the vinyl seats in the cab of the ute. 'You'll have to stay in the car.'

She turned to the window and crumpled her brow in disgust, in impatience.

'You're right,' she said.

So much for that strategy because even now, when I'm doorknocking by myself, I can't seem to chalk up much interest. More than one person is disappointed to find I'm not handing out information about the Lions Club Carols by Candlelight. Even the people I know aren't being that responsive. Even Rosie Lunt. She grimaces when she opens the door and for a horrible second I think she's glanced into my soul and seen what I've been up to but then she clutches her chest and I see that it is pain which pulls her face.

'Rosie, what's wrong?' I say.

'Strained a muscle in my bosom, love, when I opened the chutney jar this morning.'

She takes the flyer, glances at it, then turns her back on me, taking her and her sore bosom off down the hall. I note the heaviness in her step and then it dawns on me. I could kick myself. So full of my own business. For people like Rosie – and Dad – the past isn't always a cause for celebration. How dare I stand there and ask Rosie to remember what she can't possibly forget? It's an aspect of our campaign I haven't properly considered.

All in all it's been a botched job.

Dispirited, I feel like going home but it's not quite the

comfort zone it once was either. Davey will be there and just at the minute I'm doing everything I can to avoid looking into his uncomplicated face.

Back at the car the Bride has obviously been stewing in some pretty potent juices too. I slide in behind the wheel with almost as many flyers in my hand as when we parted. She is fidgety with frustration.

'I can't believe that I'm putting all this effort into preserving my parents' and grandparents' generation. It's not natural,' she says as she reapplies some dark-green lipstick. 'I mean, I'm meant to presume they don't have anything worth keeping. I'm abnormal.' She snaps shut her compact. 'I should despise – not save – their sorry arses. I'm being radically unradical and they couldn't be more ungrateful. Dumb shits.'

Her green lips twitch and I'm surprised to see her having to blink back an angry tear.

'They *never* did anything for me.'

She makes the word go bare.

I'd like to pat her arm but her scowl forbids it.

An unnoticed girl who tried hard to please.

We drive up to Ridge Road and part-way along the back of the headland we park the car, then hike up the path to the lookout which overhangs the town. We're puffed from the effort. The Bride wrinkles up her nose with distaste and brushes at a sandstone rock to make a cleaner spot for us to sit down. Take me to the highest spot, she'd said, which was unexpected because I would never have pegged her as a bushwalker. From here you can see all the houses of Pocket ringed round the bay and cars and the black dots of people moving about.

'They look like bugs,' says the Vampire Bride. As if she wanted to squish them.

'Our timing's just bad,' I say. 'Nobody's interested so close to Christmas.'

I pick off a banksia leaf and run my finger round its scalloped edge testing the serrations, and I say to her, 'What did you want to come here for?'

'This,' she says, and she pulls the rest of the purple papers out of her carry bag.

She stands at the edge of the rock like maybe she's going to swan dive off like those blokes in Hawaii. Only she'd land on someone's roof tiles and not in the sea.

'I commend the rest of these papers that nobody wants anyway to the good citizens of Pocket Head.'

And she throws her arms up in the air and lets go of them for the wind to take.

'Make your way down chimneys, stick yourselves to windows and tumble down the streets. Find who you will,' she shouts after them.

They fly off like purple bats.

'Okay, we can go now.'

'Don't you want to watch them?'

'Nah. Let's go.'

CHAPTER EIGHTEEN
IT WAS OUT

When I picked up the phone earlier tonight Barbara Audette spoke into my ear. Out of the blue. She said she wanted to chat about the ironing and by the way she's read our flyer and thinks she has some very interesting information to give. Things she thinks Bim shouldn't edit. 'He loves telling tales.' The words dripped off her tongue. And then she purred, 'Why don't you come round.'

I said, 'What about tomorrow?'

'I mean now,' she purred again.

I was defensive. I blurted more firmly, 'How about tomorrow.'

In the quiet on the telephone there was a crossed line and I could hear an argument between a man and a woman, rising and dropping out among the static.

'That would be fine,' she said.

Receivers clicked and steam came out our ears, hers as well as mine.

I'm furious. Also I feel sick. And shocked. But I am genuinely furious. She's been and left *another* basketful of ironing, she *still* hasn't got the message.

And I do feel sick.

But forget all that, it pales to nothing. All hell has broken loose.

Davey is running amok.

He pounces through the doorway of each room of the house yelling, 'I know you're here, when I find you I'm going to kill you, you bastard.'

As he goes he's got his weapon raised, his hand clutching the toe of a best Florsheim shoe, the size 11 heel weighty as a hammerhead and poised to strike. It could leave a dent in a man's skull that would fit a pomegranate.

'Davey,' I'm yelling out, 'calm down! Stop it.'

I'm fearful of what harm he'll do, what damage he'll cause.

'Davey, let him go,' I plead.

'No! I'm going to settle this once and for all.'

Every light in the house gets snapped on and off, doors slam.

'For God's sake, let him go.'

I have visions of lampshades being smashed, curtains wrenched from runners, furniture buckling under his weight, all in the mad scramble to land a pulverising blow on the head of a little cricket. It will die but we'll become refugees with only bedrolls on our backs, forced to walk away from the wreckage of our war-zoned home.

We have been kept awake for two nights running by the leg-rubbing song of this small creature. It's not so much me, I can block it out, don't mind its tune, but it's driving Davey mad. He's convinced himself it's singled him out for persecution. It doesn't seem entirely likely that an insect would make a conscious decision to torment a large man. He says it's possessed by the devil. We go to bed and there's no noise and then as soon as we turn the light off it starts up. Davey's had the light flicking on and off enough to turn us epileptic but he can't catch it out. He's emptied two aerosol cans of Baygon throughout the house and still no good. If we don't die of sleep deprivation we'll die of chemical poisoning. If there ever was a chance of us having children there's no chance now.

'Just sleep with the light on,' I say.

'I can't. I can't sleep with the light on,' he whinges.

We turn the light off – there's a full fifty seconds of glorious silence. Davey's eyes flutter closed gratefully, the tension starts to drain away from his face – and then it goes again, brighter, stronger, higher pitched than ever.

'Mongrel!' Davey hurls a pillow through the dark towards a guessed location but the cricket doesn't miss a beat and sings on.

Davey's demented.

'Stop it, calm down,' I try again.

Now he's got my cobweb broom and he's bashing at every wall and ceiling and ramming it in corners though there's nothing to be seen and, with the lights on, nothing to be heard. In the dining room the light fitting swings as he swipes past with the stick.

'Davey, you're going crazy – just imagine it's not there.'

'Imagine this, imagine that, that's all you ever do, Lal. And look where it's got you – nowhere!'

He pauses.

In the new quiet he rocks on his toes. Buffeted by the surprise of what he's said. He might have made more sense than he meant to and he's confused as to whether this reflects on him or me or both of us.

He hesitates. Looks to come to a slow decision – whatever the consequences he will go forward. 'Lal?'

I swallow hard.

And then I say with a weak smile, 'You're the one who *imagines* this cricket is the devil incarnate.'

'FUCK THIS,' Davey roars and he chucks the cobweb broom aside. 'I'm sleeping in the boat.'

The drop light over the dining room table swings, a pendulum of light and shade crossing my face. Tick-tocking across time and space from twenty-five years ago come voices muffled behind a bedroom door in a house where disagreements were rare. Mum's voice edgy, Dad's placating, backwards and forwards, light and shade. Her voice rising. His still mumbling low, 'It doesn't matter, whatever you think.' Her voice shrill, frustration and tears, 'But what do *you* think? Tell me *something!* Don't just give in!'

Light and shade.

I go to bed.

Worn out, worn thin. Gone numb. My house is a mess but I don't care. I shut my eyes, willing a dream to come and take me some place warm and deep. I lie there and lie there, but no dream comes. The cricket sings.

I turn the flowers back, it feels like opening an envelope; I turn the counterpane of flowers back onto Davey's empty side of the bed. There is nothing to be had in this room. No sleep. At the window with the curtains parted round me like a nun's veil there's no breeze. But from far away over, a long way over, I can hear the sea. Its shush and boom comes if I hold my breath. The lawn is empty except for rust falling on outdoor furniture.

I will go for a walk.

I am walking. Through the town in my nightie. With a cardigan slung round my shoulders and my cracked heels hanging over the edges of a pair of scuffs. I follow the hollow call of the surf, it seems the only thing to do, taking slow steps up the hill. The houses, with their dark sloping yards, are all tucked in. I imagine all the people I know in this town and how they'll be sleeping: Davey, self-exiled and finally unconscious, with his mouth open and the soft eye of his dick snoozing out of the fly in his pyjama pants; Rosie Lunt lying neat as a pin with the covers pulled up to her chin; Question Mark Man dangled like a spider over the arms of his vinyl chair in front of the TV, and Black Dog curled nose to tail twitching with dreams; the oysterman turned to the wall in a foetal pose and muttering the echo of a Methodist prayer; Viv in an apple-green negligee facing away from Ray but with one foot kicked back and hooked over his ankle; Dad, maybe asleep in his clothes, but not forgetting his ritual with the pillows – the two of them laid carefully end to end under the blankets, like sausage meat in pastry, to fill the place where Mum had been; Janet Constable and Iris and Bertie Marchant sprawled in an exhausted threesome. The whole town snores. How do they all stay wedged in their beds when it seems a careless nudge has tipped the world on its side and everything of mine is tumbling out of cupboards?

I am the only sleepwalker.

The kerb and guttering give way to gravel and crumble-edged bitumen. Christmas lights blink in the lounge room window of the last house before the crest. Over the hill, a salt-heavy mist hangs in the air. I can taste it on my lips. Houses sprinkle down to a fringe near the beach. The car park at the surf club floats ahead, street lights leaning over it. It's a deserted sporting arena, jewel-flecked with broken glass and flattened beer bottle tops, confettied with condom packets.

I take the dark track through the dunes. The world at night, without colour, is a muffled place. The only thing for sure is the grey-white foam of the surf, its treacherous lace strung right the way up the beach. I would not swim in the dark. It would make me feel like a lost soul to swim in the dark.

I sit in the damp sand well back from the water, hunkered down with my nightie pulled over my knees. Crack, boom, boom of the surf. But I have company. Up at the Heights there's a dull glow of orange coming from one of the cliff-top houses. I bet Barbara Audette's behind that light, smoking endless cigarettes in her cathedral gloom, watching the waves and shadows as I do.

She's waiting with me.

We are awake together on the night the whole town sleeps as if it's taken a potion.

We'll wait for daybreak.

I pick up a driftwood stick, it's both smooth and gnarled. Polished by ocean journeys but not transformed, still wood, still once part of a tree.

How does Bim sleep?

Morning.

Col and Davey and Ray and Viv play tennis together once

a month. At home I struggle through my regular jobs then pack a thermos, cut cake and put it in a tin, load up a basket, and amble off to be a dutiful spectator. So tired I'm in a cloud of my own personal fog.

I'm sitting in the tennis shed. It smells of old tea leaves. Outside, the tennis court is brilliant, hit by the sun like an axe blow. Inside, the shade of the shed is dark, hot black.

'*Come on, it was in.*'

I've got my elbows on the graffiti-carved picnic table and my hands are cupped around my face and my fingertips are pushing up the skin at the corners of my eyes to keep them open.

'*Ray, darling, you're a jerk. Serve.*'

My eyes feel grit-prickled. Tired.

'*It was in.*'

Every now and then my eyes blink and I hear them crackle and sting in my ears.

'*I'm telling you it was in, Viv. How could you see, you're at the net with your back to the baseline.*'

It's a sort of welcome torture, making myself stare into the glare.

'*I am capable of turning my head, Ray.*'

'*It whistled past your ears.*'

'*And then it whistled out. Now serve!*'

Their voices go up and down like a game of snakes and ladders.

We used to play.

We used to push the red and yellow counters backwards and forwards through school holidays and rainy afternoons the whole year I turned seven. The snakes had leery eyes and curly blue forked tongues.

'It was nearly in.'

'Nearly in is out.'

I hated those tongues.

'It doesn't matter, Viv. Give him the let.'

They licked after the counter, those tongues, even when you'd managed to avoid the squares which fenced their heads.

'No. I'm not giving him anything.'

It made you shiver with relief to slip past.

'Come on, we're just standing here getting sunburnt.'

You moved up the ladders with a firm fast diagonal ...

'Christ, fer fuck's sake give him the point.'

... and you slid reluctantly down the slow curves of the snake's back ...

'The whole point?'

... until you dripped off the thin tip of the tail to the bottom of the board.

'Davey, I don't want the whole point, I just want to play a let.'

It made Mum laugh. They didn't scare her. If she landed on a snake then the longer the better. As if any sort of action was better than none at all. I wonder if she still thinks that now.

'It was out.'

'Outish. Let him get away with it.'

Without fail, when I landed on trouble I felt the suck of disappointment.

'Don't mutter "let him get away with it," he's my husband and he's not getting away with anything.'

Over the course of travelling the blue-and-white checked squares the game was meant to even up.

'Ask the independent umpire. Lal, what do you think?'

I think the ladders are getting shorter than the snakes.

'Lal, you saw the point, was it in or out?'

I blink my eyes. The grit of no sleep stings again. I hold them shut for a long time. When I open them the players are white blurred shapes wavering like mirage heat in front of me. It's my pupils contracting for the sun that makes them dance.

'What about it, Lal? You saw it all.'

My vision straightens. My friends, my husband, they are turned to me and waiting.

'Well?'

They seem strangely arranged on the tennis court like actors on a stage.

'It was out,' I say.

Amid complaints and compliments over the decision I gather myself up. I don't know where I'm going but I'm walking, away from the courts.

I'm a fair way along Community Road when a car swings in front of me and pulls over. Bim's black BMW. It kicks up a pall of roadside dust which drifts and settles on me.

He gets out of the car.

'I'm sorry,' he says with a laugh, referring to the grit orbiting round me and trying to wave it aside. 'I've been looking for you.'

He brushes some dust from my cheek.

'Are you alright?' he says.

'Yeah, fine.'

He touches me on the elbow.

'I'm fine.'

He's waiting.

'Come and see me,' says Bim. 'At Five Wells, at the yard. I'm on my way there now.'

I shake my head no. Just a small shake no.

It's my turn to touch him on the arm.

'But, thank you,' I say.

I know where I'm going now.

CHAPTER NINETEEN
QUICKSAND

You should never be too blasé about some things and one of them's quicksand. Hence my churning guts when I see that Barbara Audette has a great big patch of it in her kitchen. She's standing on the other side of it with a smirk and a raised eyebrow wondering if I'll dare to cross. I could hang onto the benchtops and work my way round or blunder straight in, up to my thighs, my neck, my ears, in the cold sick of quicksand. And which approach would she admire the most? 'You choose, you choose,' says her grin. She may or may not pass me a rotted stick or toss out a liana vine just beyond my reach. She's gloating from the safety of a perimeter of stainless steel. The shrunken smudge of her reflected back from countless surfaces. Everywhere a little blur of her.

'Glad you could make it, Lal,' she says, 'so we can have a little talk about your society – and Bim.' She pops a Jatz and cheese whole into her mouth, lassoing a broken piece of biscuit with her tongue as if it's a live quail wriggling to be free. She turns back to the bench to cut more cheese.

'And the ironing,' I say.

It's the best I can manage.

She goes to the fridge, as big as would do a restaurant, and brings out an apple. Peels it with the cheese knife. I am hungry, which is curious but I am not offered food.

'Ah yes, the ironing,' she says. 'If there's been a ... mis-understanding ... I'm sure you're not to blame.'

I can't claim to know Barbara Audette very well, hardly at all, really, but this wolfing down of foodstuffs just doesn't seem in character. She's meant to have class. She parts the apple in one slice as if cleaving a head, and tucks in, not bothering to remove the core.

'I do it as a favour,' I say, keeping my tone bland.

'But I know how you're fond,' she says, still chewing the apple and returning to the fridge, 'of performing favours.'

My stomach rumbles.

'Bim is too, but with him there are always strings at-tached. Over the years I've learnt to be on my guard about favours. I prefer to know where I stand, don't you?'

When she reappears from behind the big fridge door she's carrying a plate with a whole roasted chicken on it. It's a number fifteen.

My mouth waters, my stomach rumbles again.

She laughs, shakes her head. 'Bim's such a liar.' She says it as if she's the proud mother of a naughty boy. 'He's very good at it, does everything well. When he lies, do you know how you can tell?'

I shake my head with more than just lack of knowledge.

'Don't look at his eyes – you'll believe them – watch his hands. His hands go speckled with rash. I think it's handy you know that, you being in the society. And watch out for the telephone. If he knows you know, he'll save his biggest lies to tell you by telephone.'

'But the ironing,' I say and I'm talking to the chicken, 'is just something I do to help.'

'He loves the way you do his shirts,' says Barbara, tearing a drumstick from the bird. 'I never did them crisply enough, apparently.' She takes a bite. 'Bim's always been careful about appearances.'

'Appearances can be important,' I say back.

She talks on quickly, 'He fixed a football match once, for a substantial sum. Easy to do when you're the kicker. Nobody knew – who would suspect the man who loved the game most of betraying it? But he wanted to be successful in all areas, including money. So he robbed Peter to pay Paul. Appearances. It goes to show, doesn't it?'

I sit there blankly. I am mesmerised by the drumstick she waves round, a little lump of meat attached by skin flaps, up and down, she could be Spanish dancing with a handled castanet.

I don't reply.

'Don't you believe me, Lal?' asks Barbara, impatient now. 'Or do you condone cheating?' And she tosses the drumstick with a flourish as if it's a bouquet I must catch. But I've mistaken her aim which is accurate after all; it crashes into a pet bowl near the pantry door.

I don't reply.

Barbara is empty handed.

I don't reply.

She stares at me. Daring.

I stare back. May as well. I don't know what else to do.

Barbara hoists an eyebrow higher.

I keep mine flat.

My face is as dumb as the moon.

Barbara teeters.

She opens her mouth to speak and sees mine twitch more firmly shut.

Nothing comes out.

She falters.

And caves in.

Her chest hollows like she's lost a couple of ribs and finally she says quietly, 'There are certain marital duties – like the ironing – that I don't mind contracting out. Under strict conditions. I've done it before.'

We stop and blink at each other.

Horrified, I take evasive action and say the only thing I'm able to say.

'May I …?

'What?'

'Have a sandwich?'

'Why, yes, of course.' She brushes a crumb from her blouse and wipes the corners of her mouth in such a dainty way that my faith in her classiness is almost restored. She puts a clean knife in my hand, 'May as well have my chicken too.'

How is this happening?

Barbara butters bread for me, gets pepper and salt and mayonnaise, asks me if I want lettuce.

'There's no reason why we shouldn't get on,' she says. 'We could give it a trial of, say, two months?'

I do want lettuce. I shred it delicately with the big knife.

'How do you feel about that?'

I feel bizarre. And now I've let the bizarreness in it's rushing, like sea water, between my ears.

She pours us each a tall glass of orange juice. Freshly squeezed.

I cut the sandwich into triangles.

I have to put a stop to this.

'No,' I say, with all the forthrightness that I can muster, 'that's not what I had in mind.'

Barbara bites her lip and gives a startled glance – she's got the wrong idea and thinks I'm taking the upper hand. Tiny lines of age hidden in layers of face powder pull at the corners of her mouth and I'm ashamed.

I was hankering for some little thing more from life, that's all, and when it bumbled by I took it. Bim asked. I said alright. I never looked towards an end, let alone this end, me sitting here with Barbara in the too real – surreal – wreckage.

'Barbara,' I say, 'you're alright now. I won't be doing anymore ironing. You're okay.'

She nods, and then to herself and not to me she pulls the purse strings of her lips to mutter, 'If only I could take an axe to Liberty.'

When I say, 'How do you stand all this?' and make my arms spread out to give a shape to the perplexity, she knows exactly what I mean.

She shrugs her shoulders. 'I've been weak in more ways than I care to tell. And I've been too long in captivity.'

We drink our juice.

I offer Barbara a corner of my sandwich but she declines. It's a shame because it's the most flavoursome chicken sandwich I've ever eaten in all my life.

Barbara gets up and flips open the door of the dishwasher, pulls out the empty racks. The machine looks like it's hardly ever used. We put the few things into it. She rearranges some stuff I've stacked in the wrong way. She looks tired. I remember her telling me she'd been a student. I'd like to have seen her then – young and keen and alive to the knowledge of ancient times.

'Maybe you'd like to join the Historical Society?' I say.

She laughs.

There's a noise from somewhere within the house. Barbara tilts her head to it and I see her toughening again. It's Bim. We hear his scratching progress down the stairs and across the living room.

'In here, darling,' calls Barbara. She takes a purple Historical Society flyer from the benchtop near the coffee maker and folds it in half neatly, deliberately, and gives it to me. 'Don't take it too seriously,' she says. 'He really isn't all he's cracked up to be.'

When Bim enters the kitchen and sees Barbara and me here together not even the tiniest flicker of surprise crosses his green eyes. And that does it for me. It makes me think that if I ever had to iron another pile of his shirts I'd return them complete with scorch marks.

'You said you'd be much later, Bim,' says Barbara, giving him a pecking kiss. 'But since you're here I think you should tell Lal a thing or two. You should confess. Tell her the truth about Girlie Tyler.'

CHAPTER TWENTY
WHAT SORT OF FISH?

I come in from the bus and dump my stuff on the kitchen table and get stuck straight into the jobs. Put away the lettuce and carrots and cucumber – a Lebanese one I've bought today, they say they don't make you burp. Portia, at work, wants to know when they'll invent a digestible capsicum. She hopes not too soon because she doles it on thick and then piles on the onions when a pain-in-the-arse customer orders salad sandwiches.

'This sandwich is made to last, you bastard,' she says under her breath, sniffing back onion tears.

I arrange the colours of fruit in the fruit bowl just so. You can see your face in the apples and the mangoes smell like Tahiti. The daisies in the vase on the windowsill have given up the ghost, heads bent, petals collapsed, a crop of shabby lampshades. I'll fling them out and pick some fresh before I put the dinner on. Lamb chops I think I'll cook. Davey likes to drown them in tomato sauce. Wipes his face on the serviette but forgets his hands wandering on the tablecloth in red smears.

I pluck the flower scissors out of the mess of the utensil drawer and go into the garden.

Saturday afternoon when Barbara had made him tell the story, Bim took a bottle of Heineken beer out of the fridge and we made our way to the living room. He leaned against the window, framed by ocean with a frill of surf pestering at his neck. I wanted to pull him back. It's a dangerous habit leaning on the nothing like that. Barbara and I sat upright on the couch, like some sort of tribunal.

'I can't do it,' said Bim, and his complaint made damp hot puffs upon the glass. 'Girlie fed me that story. *Me*, along with everyone else – and I twisted myself to fit it.' His lips turned down with bitterness. In appeal, he turned his shoulders to us, but his open stance was met with silence. He tried again. 'To contradict that story is to contradict me. Why do you think I go to so much trouble shoring it up?'

I wasn't meant to have a speaking role and there was no chance that Barbara would yield.

'Bim,' she said, 'it's no big deal.' She slid some butter into her voice to grease the steel, 'Don't worry. Lal and I have come to … an understanding. She won't tell.'

I could see what she was doing now, she was cementing us all together.

'You never know,' added Barbara. 'Telling the truth puts things back in perspective, it might even be a relief.'

Bim turned his profile towards the headland and Black Angel Cove. It took him a long time to begin.

He said when rescuers found Girlie she was on her hands and knees like a dog. She was licking the sandstone cliff where a few drips of freshwater trickled down. She had her eyes shut, lapping it up like she was in heaven but her tongue was covered in grit. When the rescuers tried to bundle her up she clawed at them and clawed at rock. They left that part out of the newspaper reports. She was meant to be a surviving hero. And it wouldn't do to tell about a woman behaving like an animal.

'Sounds understandable though,' I'd said.

But it seems that in order to make it to the beach, when she'd been in the sea, she'd grabbed hold of some passing wreckage. Except it was already occupied.

My bunch of flowers is full enough, it'll do. You can only think about the shipwreck story for so long, before you need to shake the shiver off your back.

I go inside and get the dinner ready. I get the meat out of the fridge. I used to wonder how we could eat the red butcher's writing on the fat of the chops; was it safe to eat when your mother was always saying get that pen out of your mouth and then there she was cooking up inky words for your dinner. And what were the words you were eating anyway? They didn't make sense, some sort of slaughter-man's code. A red stamp in place of oily wool. Afterwards I drew on the paper they came wrapped in.

Davey comes in asking what's for tea and leaving boot prints on the floor round the stove as he lifts pot lids.

'Mint sauce for the peas?' He's checking just because I accidentally ran out once and in disappointment he drove eight miles with one headlight for a fresh bottle when the corner shop was shut. I shoo him off to the shower and wipe the floor. Pushing the cloth round and round. The pattern on the lino is intricate enough to mean nothing.

Bim said he never knew until old age loosened her tongue. 'She told me that boy's calf muscle fitted the palm of her hand like it was made for it.' Bim reckoned he couldn't pick up a wrench in the workshop without its weight and balance making pictures – white skin, black sea – without him also clasping a soon-to-be-drowned boy.

In her dotage she'd bragged.

She loved that night and hated it as well. Loved it because she'd never felt such power and never would again. The power of the elements raging, her power to resist, and the power of her soaring strength of will over death and another human life. And she knew she'd do it over.

She had snatched into the dark at a white leg hanging from a raft of junk, had dragged her way up the body of the young man suckered on there. She dragged her way up his thin body and pulled, and clawed skin, clawed splintered timber, and the boy whimpered as they ploughed, now half submerged with her added weight, through the turmoiled water. His grip shifted and the raft lurched and she shuffled to gain a firmer hold and he was gone. She saw wraith hands reaching out of water plucking at thin air for anything, hands without a head, and then the head surfaced and an arm reached, four fingertips, a thumb for a pincer, pulling down on a corner of her raft. She turned and planted her palm across his crown in a firm bishop's blessing and pushed him under.

I'm beginning to see the many ways that history gets censored, and the many whys.

After dinner, the suds in the washing-up water are ringed with beaches of red scum, a by-product of waste tomato sauce. Davey loved his dinner. I pull the plug and there's that horrible noise as it all gets sucked away. When I was a kid it frightened me.

'I'm just going to fish the twilight,' I call out through open doors. There's no reply. Just the gibberish of the TV. A Funniest Home Videos special. I make the sounds of departure.

Walking down the road to the jetty I look back at our neglected house. A shaft of light from a split in the overcast closing sky singles it out. It's a celestial ray, beamed up and bounced down from Hollywood. The side wall I'd once tried to paint is blazing bright. You can't pick the line between the new paint and the old, you can't see the brush hairs, the cracks, the bubbling imperfections, from here.

At the jetty I dangle my legs over the edge. I'm not fishing. Didn't even bring any bait. The water is a sloppy flat grey, like an old woman's cardigan. Further out, the yellow of a sandbar looms under it. It's almost the dead-end bottom of the tide. The wrong time to fish. I do not have the heart to throw in a hook anyway. I don't want to catch anything. I don't want to take a fish from its home tonight. Instead, I'd like to be one, nosing about in the gloom, not attached to anything, not stuck to earth, but free to glide through impersonal water. Tonight, I would be a plain fish if I could choose. No need to be flashy. The body of a blunt-nosed, round-eyed mullet would do. A mostly vegetarian who does not cause trouble.

But on a different night, and faced with different circumstances, stakes that were dire, I might choose to be a more ruthless fish. Who can say?

Bim's got it wrong. He thinks Girlie Tyler was a coward, and he's ashamed. He's got hero on the brain – and I see now why he worships Liberty. A figurehead from a junked schooner. Why he would wish to kiss her salt-timbered lips, be a Romeo to her wooden Juliet, touch her fingertips, touch palm to palm, hoping that her hand which lights the sea would light them both – animate her frozen grain and wash from him the pore-filling grime of the monkey wrench and the football fields of dirt he's wallowed in for boys-own glory, and a dollar or two on the side.

He's in love with a wooden woman because her purity is untouched by real life. She's unchanged.

Maybe he'd rather his grandmother had nobly died but then, where would he be? He's got hero on the brain and doesn't see the great and awful courage required to be selfish enough to survive.

The thing that chills is what sort of fish did my mum choose to be? And why?

'It is a still night for you, Lal?'

It's Question Mark Man. As I turn, my face is almost plastered by Black Dog's tongue, and Question Mark's grey-trousered body stands close and over me.

It's a good question.

Is it a still night for me? It's still except for the dull thud of my heartbeat.

'You don't seem well?'

'I'm kind of sad tonight.'

'There is something I can do?'

I wish that was a statement. I shake my head.

'Make the wind blow,' I say, trying to lighten things up. 'From any direction you fancy, make the wind blow.'

'I could try,' says Question Mark Man puffing out his oval cheeks, 'but I do not think summoning the elements is one of my long suits? You should ask the elderly gentleman?' And he inclines his oblong head towards the oysterman's bay and there's the old man in the distance, dragging a fallen tree branch to the woodheap beside his house and pausing mid-step to look up at a white cockatoo wheeling and screeching across the valley.

Question Mark Man says, 'There is a man of much experience?'

'But I can't call out all that way,' I say. 'Besides, he doesn't speak to anyone.'

'Even when you speak to him?' says Question Mark Man.

I shrug my shoulders.

'Then I will do what I can do, Lal?' And he flaps his arms up and down at his sides in a gesture that indicates he's resigned to his task, but also suggestive of the pumping of a bellows.

Black Dog barks.

It's dark when I get home. Davey has gone to bed. I sit up a little while and then turn in too.

I lie between the freshly laundered sheets, crisp, just like they were always crisp when I was a little girl and they smelled of washing-powder lemon.

There was a time when I was maybe eight years old; sheets flapping on the clothes line and me sitting underneath pretending I'm in a Bedouin tent. As the line drifts round to the nudge of a desert zephyr I see Mum and Dad through the gaps in my tent walls. They are sitting on the garden bench near the back door. A plank is missing from the seat and their bottoms bulge down filling the gap.

Mum's bottom is neat, a floral dress with a grey background, and Dad's is a larger longer bulge of checked shorts. They are sitting in Sunday morning sun. Mum is cutting Dad's fingernails. She is quick and deft.

I am playing with the picnic basket got out of the hall cupboard and I have its contents spread out across the grass. There are anodised beakers, a bit scratched, and plastic plates, dull-coloured and brittle. I have collected flowers and weeds and am arranging them as Arab food.

Now Dad is cutting the nails of Mum's right hand, the ones she can't do easily for herself. She is looking out over the back fence past Clayburns' rooftop, over and away to the ridge and beyond. She's in a trance. Dad has Mum's arm resting on his leg, tucked into his thigh, and he holds up each slim finger to the scissors snipping gently, gently. He goes so carefully and so slowly it's like he does not want to stop. Does not want to finish the last finger knowing he will have to give back her hand.

I see now that he loves her too much.

And I recognise that look on Mum's face as one of longing – for space away. It was a look I think Dad saw but would not acknowledge, preferring, instead, to hang onto a happiness myth.

In a way, they're not dissimilar, Dad and Bim. They gripped their stories so tight they couldn't let go and it imprisoned them.

Mum looking out past the neighbour's rooftop. Trying to make herself airless to the touch of Dad's large hands. Between snips, the quick guilty tilt of Dad's head as he steals glances of her.

That mad old dentist's father could have been right after

all. Not about Mum, but about Dad. I hear his hissing words, *Your father watched.*

The tent walls blow and turn and screen my parents off and it's just me with my picnic feast for absent Arabs.

I lie between my freshly laundered sheets but I can't sleep. I get up. I walk the floors of the dark house, room to room. I can't settle. I wait for, pray for, the first muscle-flexing gusts of a southerly to rattle at the windows. But Question Mark Man musters nothing.

CHAPTER TWENTY-ONE
AULD ACQUAINTANCE

'I come from Cockatoo Station, love, way out west,' she says with her fat woman's asthma. 'I filled those wide blue skies with song.'

Her bosom sparkles catch the light as if the way-out-west sun had slammed into her. She laughs a wheezy smoker's, singer's, husky laugh.

'And I've done pubs and clubs across the country ever since and I love 'em all. Belt out the standards until dawn, have a few drinks, cup my hand round the back pocket of a pair of moleskins, the world's my oyster.'

She's dragging on her Rothman's cigarette as if it's the force of life. The smoke curls around her bleach and perm. Her earrings swing to the band's beat as she turns her head towards some new distraction. She's on a break until her next set. She is tired, but she is showbiz.

'Get her another vodka,' I hiss to Davey.

The poker machines clang and rattle change.

It's New Year's Eve and the club is really jumping. The tickets promised a big night at the splurging price of fifty-five dollars a double. Lottie Lorrel, Vince Carlisle, and the Sweet Sixteen Sensational Sixties Band.

Lottie Lorrel picks the slice of lemon out of her empty glass with long white varnished nails and when she puts it back it's only a thin smile of rind. Doesn't even wince with the sourness. She catches me looking and laughs, 'You've gotta look after yourself when you're on the road – don't wanna get scurvy. Thanks, love,' and she nods businesslike when Davey slides a fresh drink across the table through a slalom course of beer coasters.

She's nice. She's very friendly. When Ray and Viv got up to dance she just plonked herself down and started chatting. She's quite famous. She's been on the TV. Vince Carlisle has too but only when it was first invented. He's onstage now, doing an up-tempo medley, the dance floor's full of jitter-buggers and jive steppers, you should see the retirees go, they're the best dancers. The sweat's pouring off Vince, he wants to be careful, his hair's slipping. Lottie notices too, I think, because she laughs out a clump of cigarette smoke and says, 'Better get up and do my bit.' Bertie Marchant nips in and waylays her, holding out his ticket and asking her to autograph it. Bertie's looking very smart tonight, if a little overdressed, in a dinner suit. Lottie butters him up good and proper and he beams and puffs his chest out and by the time she goes he looks like he'd swim the English Channel for her.

He starts talking to us, Davey gives him a ribbing about being a stage-door johnny, and Bertie asks have we heard about the oysterman and, of course, we have. It's the news of the night and everyone knows about it. Bertie says he saw Gaynor Daley here earlier and she said her kids were delighted the old man was dead since they thought he was the bogeyman. 'Maybe now I can get them to sleep with the light off,' she'd said.

Davey says Moody's sitting up at the bar now nursing a rum and Coke. It was Moody who found him. He was coming back from the Co-op, midmorning, when he saw this big star-shaped thing floating in the water. Took his boat in for a closer look and there was the oysterman. Dead as a doornail. Floating in the outer reaches of the lease, a bare six inches of water between his back and a bed made of oysters. Like levitation, Moody said. Looked like an old wizard, had a boathook in one hand. And a piece of paper was pasted to his left ankle between boot-top and trouser cuff, for all the world as if the old man had gone out wearing one bright-purple spat. Moody fished him out. The police found his dinghy, it had drifted clean away to knock on a straggle of rocks near the opening to the sea.

Davey tells Bertie that Moody reckons the old man had a heart attack and fell overboard. Davey, who likes to tease his weak stomach with a gory detail, had asked Moody if the old man had swollen up. 'Nup,' said Moody. But the oysterman had his eyes open. No expression, no surprise or fear, just a blank.

'Poor old bugger,' says Bertie, and he looks a bit deflated. Like he's not Lottie Lorrel's virile swimming champion anymore. I think he's momentarily reminded he might not be too far off old buggerdom himself. But he makes a conscious effort to perk up, 'Better get back to the ladies,' and he gives me a charming bow.

Davey asks me to dance and we push our way onto the parquetry. He likes to get a little pissed before he's game enough to get out there but once he's underway he makes a big statement, mixing the tango in with the twist, concocting a finger-pointing disco style – 'Watch out for Mr

Marshall's eye!' – then the of Pride of Erin and a dash of Elvis hula-hooping hips. We're just about to topple into Bobby Goggle-Eyes's tower of collected glasses when we're back into a tango, we do the dip. Davey's got a black drink straw between his teeth, 'My God, you're ravishing,' he says, before we spin away to burrow down into the samba. You really have to know someone well to follow a lead like this. Next thing I'm twirled off and flung into a plastic chair, knickers showing, and he's picked up Rhonda Meekle, he's a dreadful ham, she's begging off, she's too shy, too flat of foot, but he won't have a bar of it, he will invent a step for her, will hold her off the ground so she won't have to do a thing. I think she should wear a crash helmet. Davey's once-a-year, one-off dancing spree could end at any time.

I sneak off, I don't want to be the one who has to scream out 'Call the ambulance'. As I weave between narrow table gaps and bump past seated people yelling into each other's ears the music changes and the Sweet Sixteen move on a decade into the 1970s. Lottie Lorrel pumps out 'Nutbush City Limits'. The retirees leave the danger of the dance floor to Davey and the other 'youngies'.

In the Ladies, Rene Levique, seventy-one years young, eyes asparkle with music and vermouth, mops herself up and repowders her wrinkles. Cubicle doors bang, the queue shuffles forward. Gossip and chat. The sweet smell of mari-juana drifts in through a high louvred window. Some kids must be hanging out the back. Rene snaps her make-up purse shut, gives herself a wink in the mirror, does a little spin and a silver shoe slide in front of the washbasin. On her way out she addresses the whole room, 'Girls, I think I'm in love!'

Whistles and cheers.

'And what about you?' says Viv to me, under the cover of the toilet clamour. I shake my head gently. Give a coy smile.

At half past eleven the band takes a break and Vince Carlisle, flapping his silver-sequinned coat to cool down, pants into the microphone, 'My, my, you people really know how to have fun.' He puts on his best MC's voice in between sips from a glass of water. 'And now for the official part of the evening.' There follows the drawing of the lucky door prize, a best-dressed award, a worst-dressed award. In the pauses, as recipients make their way to the stage, Vince licks his lips. He's got a bright-pink tongue like a dog's dick. It keeps popping out of his mouth, now exploring the air, now retreating.

Davey wins a meat tray of pork for his impression of Fred Astaire and he holds it over his head for the crowd as if it's the Melbourne Cup.

'We would have given your partners a prize,' puffs Vince, 'but they're still in traction.'

'Blame it on the bossa nova!' yells out some wag.

The punters love it.

'It's twenty to midnight,' says Vince, 'so avoid the stampede and top up your drinks at the bar.'

I avoid the stampede entirely and skirt out the back to the dining room with the meat tray. There's a trotter in it with a sprig of parsley between its toes – what sick butcher did that for decoration? – and Davey's Old Boys Network want to get it out of the packet and do tricks with it. I'm hoping Mai will keep the tray safe in her fridge for me. The dining room is cleared except for the debris of paper party hats and a few rubber shreds of burst balloons, but through the swinging double doors, the kitchen is in chaos. Good-natured, tired-to-the-bone chaos. All the staff have tea towels in their hands or washing-up gloves on but they're sipping champagne and joking along like they're on holidays.

'Mai,' I say, 'you've all got to get out of here soon and go inside for the countdown. Let me help. You can't miss it.'

'Looks bad,' she giggles, 'but there's not much more to do.'

She's sitting on a benchtop, strictly against her own rules, with one shoe off and she's rubbing her toes, 'My God, I will die entirely if I have to serve one more Sweet and Sour Pork.' And then she screams and collapses in a gale of laughter and points at my meat tray, 'Don't tell me – you want rice!'

We put the pack on a shelf in her coolroom and as we're shutting the big door Mother Lin appears. She pulls a folded rectangle out from the pocket of her apron and it sighs in soft crinkles as her old hands unmake it back into a page. She passes it to me. The writing is very beautiful, its strokes contain pictures of trees, the loops and sharp kicks of fishhooks, crosshatches of sturdy fences, overhangs of rock. They are Chinese words stacked one on top of each other, like growth notches in a stick of bamboo.

Mother Lin nods at me, take it, take it, but I shake my head, no. The paper looks old and very precious.

'She wants you to have it, Lal,' says Mai. 'For your society.'

The old lady pats my hand.

It's a letter from her great grand uncle who fished the inlet with shore nets at Coolie. 'How do you think Coolie gets its name? Mai says. 'Chinese fishermen camp there. Very

successful. They even export dried fish until those Actons
mess the business up and build a town.'

Mother Lin nods again.

Mai says the letter describes everything, better than a
Kodak picture, for the people at home. Her old uncle, a favoured uncle, did not return to China but was killed by
bandits on the Bathurst road.

'She gives him to you for safekeeping,' says Mai.

I take another look at that faded script, the patience and
control contained within it, and wonder at the courage
and enterprise of those early Chinese settlers, brave enough
to be the strangest of strangers in a strange land.

I fold the paper, kiss Mother Lin on her smooth cheek,
and usher them both through the kitchen.

We make it out into the main bar area just in time to join
in the countdown to midnight. Everyone's standing up,
some are on chairs, some on tables, craning to get a glimpse
of the television set. It's as if the TV is the oracle of
chronological truth, it wouldn't do for us to celebrate a few
seconds later than the rest of the world. Besides, we have to
check it's there, that the rest of Australia is really there. We
have to check to make sure we haven't somehow got it
wrong.

THREE … we holler.

TWO … we scream.

ONE … we're hoarse.

HAPPY NEW YEAR!

Everyone kisses everyone else hoping it's someone with
lips they don't mind, or if they do mind they try not to. Mai
even gives Bobby Goggle-Eyes a big smacker. People are
pulling down streamers and draping them on their heads

and round their necks, they're tripping up on them, trampling them into the floor. Lottie and Vince lead us all in 'Auld Lang Syne' and we link hands to make a cobbled-worm circle round the dance floor, between tables, through the poker machines and up to the bar, including everyone in the room. We warble at top volume. The strong truth of Lottie's clear voice carries us with her as we climb:

Should auld aquaintance be forgot and never brought to mi-y-ind.

We teeter and nearly crash on that last strained word, but she soars and takes us on. There's nothing vulnerable in her rendition of the song, no frailty, it's a straight path, but I notice Vince weakening, not quite concentrating, letting a tear creep into his eye, maybe he's thinking about a wife who dumped him, or a grown-up daughter who used to call him daddy.

We'll tak a cup o' kindness yet,
For auld lang syne.

And then I let go of Lottie too and I'm thinking about the oysterman floating face up in the water and how Moody found him wrapped with the purple spat of our Historical Society flyer, and I know he reached for it. He didn't have a heart attack at all, or not that sort, the one involving muscles and spasms, electrical pulses in the body's motor. He reached out for our notice in the water. Reached to gather in the purple flower blooming on the water, only to have it taken from him by the sucking current of a turning tide. A single, strange purple jellyfish of a flower. And what if it hadn't stuck to boot-top and trouser cuff? He would have missed his prize. And I'd never have known it was something worth having. I close my eyes. Wishing I could swim with the oysterman in an inlet filled with purple jellyfish. And then Lottie swoops in and picks us both up, the oysterman and me, takes us right up, dripping, and we're with her again, safe in the silver steel of her voice:

We'll tak a cup o' kindness yet,
For auld lang syne.

She holds us up to the sun, to the mirror ball, and we're dripping salt-water drops, we're in the sunlight of her grand, hard praise:

For auld lang syne.

More kisses. Cheers. A conga line forms, it seems everyone wants to keep touching each other since licence has been given. The snake gets underway. Ray and Viv are very drunk, they make the line stop and do a can-can. Legs kick and accidentally tip over empty chairs. Someone yells out, 'What about a striptease,' and the conga re-forms and slithers on, begins to pick up speed. I've got my hands on Davey's broad hips, he gives a wiggle. The line weaves past the bar and outside through the glass doors into the green verandah light and the night of a new year.

CHAPTER TWENTY-TWO
THE OYSTERMAN'S HOUSE

I've got my skirt tucked into the legs of my undies to keep it up out of the water. I'm holding the bow rope of the *Extractor* at arm's length as if the boat's a stud bull, I can't go deeper than knees or I'll get too wet. Davey drives back up the ramp and parks the trailer. The Vampire Bride stands firm on the grass as if the touch of sea water, not holy water, would cause an uncomfortable sensation if not certain death. You'd think she'd enjoy a paddle as cool relief from the day's humidity.

'I hate nature,' she calls out. 'When's it going to be over?'

I take a couple of steps to my right to avoid a fish head floating in the water, undercurrents knock it along the sandy bottom. It would have been a beauty – a jewfish. Someone's lucky. They're nice eating.

My feet make me feel a bit guilty. Flashes of pink toenail polish swim up. I keep painting them, sort of for Bim, and sort of for Davey, but mostly for me. It's a way of not dismissing what happened and a reminder that I have been wanted. Strange, but after a single infidelity, I am forever stuck with Bim as part of my marriage.

There's a scream and Davey wades towards me with the Vampire Bride slung over his shoulder.

'Put me down,' she yells, and he pauses, tempted. 'Noo, don't put me down.'

He flips her up over the side of the boat.

'She's as light as a feather, Lal,' he says. 'Better ask her home for a decent feed.'

Davey drives full bore, slamming the hull into every wave and wavelet so that I'm sure we've worn the putty from the joints between our bones. It takes us about two and a half minutes to cross the bay. He puts the fender out over the side and glides the boat in, 'You're coming at it too fast,' I say, 'slow down,' and he wrenches the gear lever into reverse to put on the brakes but the boat still hip-bumps the rickety old jetty and all its timbers judder.

'Sling that round the pole would you, love,' he says to the Vampire Bride, handing her a dirty bit of rope. She stares at it mortified.

'Oh don't worry, give it here,' and he fixes it himself.

With the engine off, the valley settles around us. The wake of the boat spools on without us until it finds the shore in a neat, sighing curl. A crow drawls in its burnt-toast voice, 'Argh, aargh.' No one moves straightaway. None of us is in that big a hurry to look in the dead man's house, though it seemed good news when, unofficially, we were told we could. Bim knows the Coolie Trustee.

'You want to see how poor people kept house round here
~~1930s?~~' the Trustee said. 'That oysterman's house is in
You might think it's worthwhile taking a
or something, for your library collection.
~~ke~~ don't remove anything.'

'Are you coming in with us, Davey?' I ask.

'Do you want me to?'

'Yes,' we both say.

From the end of the jetty, the house looks spooky, low-roofed and too battered and small to be habitable. The outbuildings and the empty chook shed are dilapidated structures too. It's a shock seeing it all up close and a bit damning to think we had neglected him so.

When we get to the oysterman's door it answers to our push and opens in to a hovel. Dirt thick on every surface, cobwebs strung from rough rafters. We shuffle in and take up spots as far away from each other as we can to create a sense of space where there is none. We seem like giants in a house, in a land, that does not belong to us. We are travellers in time and someone else's pain. Davey's eyes brim and glisten.

There's a table and three chairs, a sink with a single tap, dishes on the drainer, and a contraption for holding soap and waving it under water to make suds. Daylight shows through gaps round the window frame where it no longer meets the wall. There's a granite bench, a combustion stove, a dresser with a few chipped plates and cups. Shelves on the wall are stacked with cans: canned sausages, braised steak and onions, camp pie, carrots. Kerosene lamps. An alarm clock made out of a salmon tin. A grey furry toothbrush standing in a glass. Pans and basins hang on walls which are blackened with a hundred years of wood smoke. There's a single bed, as narrow and thin-mattressed as a stretcher, two wardrobes. There's a double bed tilted down at one corner from a broken leg.

The Bride puts her hand up under her hair to twist a earring.

Davey struggles with a catch and opens up a side window for fresh air.

He says, 'It's like the Great Depression never left.'

I can't just stand there doing nothing. Something should be done. I start tidying up.

I feel like an undertaker. I'm touching the most personal parts of this man's life. I'm putting away his washing-up left on the bench, putting it away for decency's sake, and I'm touching the forks and spoons he put in his mouth, the knife with which he spread the butter on his bread. I'm folding the tea towel which he may have used to wipe his hands and I'm hanging it over the back of a chair. I'm straightening the bedclothes on his bed to cover up the wrinkles and stains his body has made, and I'm plumping the pillow to set to rights the dent made by the weight of his head. I am changing things but I'm not tidying him away, I'm just making order, like an undertaker. I'm remaking his last place among the living. I'm putting a pair of boots together at the foot of the bed, toe by toe, heel resting by heel, I'm picking up a black plastic comb whose broken teeth are like the strings of a loom, woven with a few wires of hair, and I'm just about to find a place to put it when the Bride says, 'Look at this.'

She's sitting on the floor and her skirt is fanned round her like the wings of a black moth. She's bowed over an old metal munitions box. She holds up a photograph. It's a picture of half-a-dozen men in front of a horse and van at _____ the Merrengong iceworks. One must be a _____-piece suit and hat, and one in a white _____ delivery man, the others are workers. _____g for the camera in those days, everyone looks very serious and handsome. It's interesting how the forced smiles we now insist on almost always wreck your face.

The Bride digs out a second photo. It's of the Methodist mission boat taken at the Coolie chapel wharf, and a well-proportioned vessel she looks too. Standing on the wharf is a trio of a man and a woman and a boy. It's the oysterman when he was an oysterboy. He's got shorts on and bare legs and bare feet, his shirt looks way too big as if it's a cast-off from some strapping lad who's better fed; it might even have belonged to his father, it's so large. His face is thin and pinched and he hides behind a falling fringe of black hair. He doesn't belong to the man and woman that's for sure because their demeanour and their dress describe a whole other class and way of life, and shows they have a stake in the world. No doubt they are the Methodist missionary couple, the Reverend and Mrs Thatch. Reverend Thatch has a bible in his hand, Mrs Thatch has a satchel of books, and the oysterboy holds an apple. Although he doesn't look very comfortable between his benefactors, the oysterboy has his bare feet firmly splayed and it looks as if he's not about to run off anywhere in case he gets a chance to have a stake in the world too.

The Bride flips back to the first photo and studies the faces and then points at a worker, 'That one must be the kid's father, look, they're so alike.' And holding the photos side by side I agree, the man has the same coal colouring. Funny to think of that black-haired, black-tempered man, working among clean ice. Among blocks of white ice, with their trapped stars of concussion.

We go through the contents of the munitions box hoping

to find more photographs and especially wishing we could find one of the oysterboy's mother but there are no more, she's not there. It's the way with mothers.

Under a pile of school exercise books is a yellowed envelope containing the father's death certificate. Influenza, reads the round-noded type. Place of death, Rabbit Island Institution for the Insane. Date of death, 8th Aug, 1953.

Davey is going through the exercise books and shows us the faded lead of copied alphabets, book after book of them, as if the repetition of the letters was some sort of meditation drill:

a a a b b b c c c

'He couldn't have learnt too much at school if this is all he could manage,' says Davey.

'Well at least he knew how to write his own name,' says the Bride.

Each book has his name written on the front cover along with the year. The first, Merit brand, is labelled Michael Ennis, 1954. Interesting that he starts his new pursuit after his father's death. I imagine the oysterman as a child practising his letters in the sand with a knobbled finger of stick but being sure to write only where the tide would take away all traces of his secret. Not wanting his illiterate father to see his magic.

The oysterman's writing gets better as he goes on, the sticks of the d's stand straighter and the tails of the y's and g's become more gracefully looped, until, at last, he experiments with a word. Green.

green   green   green

In subsequent books each page is filled up with just one word, practised over and over. They're all ordinary words: hook, pin, orange, fin, hat, saw, rake, cloud. Words and words. In a Cambridge brand book he makes a quantum leap and starts to put words together in not exactly sentences but more like groups.

green   green
green   green
green   green
water

oyster catcher
oyster catcher
oyster catcher
red legs

'Sort of beautiful,' says the Bride. 'Like poems.'
    We skip ahead to the last book and read:

fish   gull   cloud
fish   gull   cloud
fish   gull   cloud
water   wind

We don't know what to make of the oysterman's words. Davey packs the books back into the trunk.
    'I wonder if the Trustee would give us these?' I say.

'We should be able to get the photos,' says the Bride, 'but what good are the books?'

I don't know.

I say, 'Just because you don't understand what a thing means doesn't mean it's not important. Imagine if they just chucked out the Dead Sea Scrolls because they couldn't read them.'

'What's so good about the Dead Sea scrolls anyway?' says Davey.

'These writings are as much a part of him as the photos, maybe more. We can't just chuck a person away.' It's silly, but for some reason I'm suddenly hot and flustered.

'Okay,' says the Bride. 'It's okay, we can ask.'

I pick up the old man's comb that I've laid aside and place it on the kitchen shelf next to the toothbrush. 'Davey,' I say, 'could you do something about the bed?'

He puts a question on his face but doesn't ask it. Goes searching for a chock to put under the broken leg. As most men do, he reaches for the nearest thing, a lump of sandstone which I suppose was used as a doorstop. I shake my head. There's a sunset in the stone and it wouldn't be right to shove its ochre colours into a permanent dark under the bed. Davey takes a small tin of beetroot and a bigger one of beans from the kitchen shelf and puts his shoulder to the bed to lift it up while he slides them in. He resurfaces with an old newspaper and a pair of socks. The bed is a nearly flat plateau.

Davey and the Bride look through the paper, it's full of the war news of 1945, they turn the fragile pages, laugh at the ads. I refold the socks turning them into each other the way Mum taught me and I open the wardrobe looking for a drawer, only it's not a wardrobe, it's a cupboard. The doors swing to reveal shelves, and arranged upon them is a strange collection. Trash. Displayed as treasure. A child's plastic ball, a McDonald's cup, a poddy mullet trap, a sail bag, a rubber glove. A chunk of polystyrene foam from a surfboard. A hair-roller, an ice-cream container with 'Date Slice' written on it. Discarded things, lost and forgotten things, once adrift, or windborne, or washed-up. Davey and the Bride put aside 1945 to come and pick over the shelves.

'I reckon this was Col's,' says Davey, and he holds up a filthy fishing hat. 'He's always losing hats.'

'Let's go shopping,' says the Bride and she flashes a battered credit card that once belonged to Bertie Marchant, only it's long expired. There's even an empty bottle of angina pills prescribed to Rosie Lunt, one under the tongue as required. If the oysterman had been successful fishing our Historical Society flyer from the water this is where it would have ended up. It seems the oysterman has garnered parts of people, found pieces of their living and brought them home. It shows he tried to stay in touch with us, he brought us home.

On a top shelf there's a woman's court shoe, paisleyed with ancient swirls of coarse white dust. I put my finger to the powder expecting it to lift to my touch but it turns out it's not dust – it's salt – bitten in and part of the leather. I lift the shoe and something slides down from the toe to the heel. A watch. Stopped at ten past four. It's my mother's wristwatch. I can see the faint glow of luminescence.

Davey looks up from examining Rosie's pill bottle in time to see me disobey the Coolie Trustee.

'Is that something for the library?' he asks.

'No,' I say. 'It's for me.'

I wade through the house and find the door.

My mother's things.

I hold the shoe tight in my left hand and clench the watch in my right, my arms stretched long as a primate's, carrying such weight.

He knew.

He knew.

The oysterman knew something and now he's dead and gone away. And I did not ask.

An image flashes of the oysterman and my mother, together, lovers, but it recedes as quickly as it's formed. Not these two, each with their separateness.

I walk, stumble, along the low-tide stink-muck shore of this ignored bay and I'm not seeing straight. The day, the inlet, is all salt and glare and I've got no peripheral vision. I'm just following the tidal stain where the high water last etched shore, following that line in the absence of any other guide and hoping it will go on forever.

I did not ask.

The end of the beach comes abruptly and I'm not ready for it. Rocks, tufted grasses and a great heap of oyster-farming junk, tarred sticks and trays and cages.

There's nowhere else to go.

Nothing else to do but sit, and look at what's in my hands.

I take a deep breath.

The shoe. So crusted and hard it might cut a foot that slipped into it now. Once it trod carpet and tapped over lino, paced domesticated bounds, until one day it stepped over.

The watch. Gold with a metal-linked band. It has a

mildewed face, hands stuck at ten past four and the date frozen in a tiny frame. It's the numerals of the date which crack me open. Twenty-three. The day Mum left was April twenty-third.

The oysterman must have known something. I could make some wild lament with the frustration of it all, cry out to heaven – but it wouldn't be honest. I'm too tired. Too suddenly old. How simple to have asked.

My mother's watch is stopped, the way a watch stops when plunged in water.

I look up to the bay and suddenly I'm seeing a different day, an autumn afternoon, still and brittle. I see a woman walking into the shallows of the inlet as if she's walking through a garden of unmowed grass, the water up to her knees, her thighs. My mother – maybe drawn towards the silvered glint of a Merrengong windowpane, a quick slice of afternoon light recurring if a particular path was kept, an angle, a line of tread adhered to. A sliver of beautiful suddenly seen one ordinary afternoon when things were a little worse than usual. And how glorious for a change to be heading towards something.

However many ways I imagine it I am not angry. Or shocked, or hurt.

Following the beautiful.

I could have done it.

I unhook myself from being a child.

I worry for her. Was she surprised when the water rose, was she afraid when her journey changed and its other destination became apparent?

Returning to that autumn day I give her something I need her to have, a friend – the oysterman – rowing towards her.

He ships his oars with a rattle that Mum can't hear and retrieves her gently from the water. The inlet drips from her in pearls. She's a still fish, done with swimming.

The shoe, the watch. It seems appropriate to rouse myself and bury Mum's shoe deep in the sand where the next king tide will wash over. She's never coming back. I sit for a long while. Grit in my fingernails.

The front door of the oysterman's house complains on its hinges.

Davey comes out.

He stands and shades his eyes, looking down the beach towards me. He shuffles, puts his hands in his pockets. He walks halfway and calls out, 'You alright?'

When I don't move he comes the rest of the way over.

He says, 'Are you alright?'

And I say I don't know.

He shifts his body to block out the sun and lends his shadow to me.

It occurs to me that I don't always appreciate many of the small, kind things he does for me, so I say to him now, 'Thank you.'

He helps me up and undoes my hand, takes the wrist-watch from it and puts it into my pocket.

'It was Mum's,' I say.

He mumbles, no words, just a comfort sound, a pigeon coo, and puts his thumb into the palm of my hand and strokes at the hard press marks printed there.

Undertaker, undertaking. Davey gently ushers me back into the oysterman's house, 'There you go, love.'

I return to my self-assigned task of tidying.

Davey and the Bride bring in photographic equipment

from the boat and start setting up. I was going to video the place but now Davey's offered to take over and the Bride's going to do still pictures.

My work helps, it makes me calm. I don't care if I'm meddling with the accuracy of our historical record because in a strange way I'm doing it to repay the oysterman and hold his hand. You see, the minute those photographic images are formed and stuck on tape or film we will have taken him under and consigned him to the past. So I'm doing this intimate tidying up to help him travel well and to hold his hand.

I wipe down the kitchen table. Tuck in the chairs. Step back to assess the clean. But it's not right – I've made a blankness, and that's not what I'm trying to achieve. I open up the cupboard doors to show off the oysterman's collection of discarded things. Bertie Marchant's credit card, Col's fishing hat, the kids' plastic ball – all the small parts of the town that the oysterman brought home. And then I remember the munitions tin. I get Davey to lift it up and I unpack its contents. Spread out the books, opening up some. Let daylight fall upon the hidden words.

low tide
low tide
low tide
turn

Reading the oysterman's poems I feel like I'm reading his last will and testament – and his bequest is the whole inlet. Any four lines would fit written on a cigarette paper, a little bit of paper thinner than thin, you could put it in your pocket and walk, a whole inlet slooshing from side to side, fathoms testing the seams.

It's a bequest that's made to Mum and me. And I can see us walking along the beach against the wind singing the words out loud together.

I think I am beginning to realise that it is probably everyone's intention to leave the best part of themselves behind.

I finish arranging the oysterman's display. I've made his history, but it's not one-sided because his history has also made us.

'Take a photo of that,' I say.

The Bride swings round her professional-looking camera.

The flash flashes, the shutter clunks.

The oysterman, Michael Ennis. My mother.

They're away.